AYN RAND is the author of *Atlas Shrugged*, philosophically the most challenging bestseller of its time. Her first novel, *We the Living*, was published in 1936, followed by *Anthem*. With the publication of *The Fountainhead* in 1943, she achieved a spectacular and enduring success. Rand's unique philosophy, Objectivism, has gained a worldwide audience. The fundamentals of her philosophy are set forth in such books as *Introduction to Objectivist Epistemology*, *The Virtue of Selfishness*, *Capitalism: The Unknown Ideal*, and *The Romantic Manifesto*. Ayn Rand died in 1982.

LEONARD PEIKOFF is universally recognized as the world's premier Ayn Rand scholar. He worked closely with Rand for thirty years and was designated by her as heir to her estate. He has taught philosophy at Hunter College and New York University. Dr. Peikoff's books include *The Ominous Parallels* and *Objectivism: The Philosophy of Ayn Rand*. He is also the co-editor of *The Ayn Rand Reader*, available in a Plume edition. For further information, you can go to his website, alshow.com.

ANTHEM

by

Ayn Rand

50TH ANNIVERSARY EDITION

With a New Introduction
and Appendix
by Leonard Peikoff

A PLUME BOOK

PLUME
Published by the Penguin Group
Penguin Group (USA) Inc., 375 Hudson Street, New York, New York 10014, U.S.A.
Penguin Group (Canada), 90 Eglinton Avenue East, Suite 700, Toronto,
Ontario, Canada M4P 2Y3 (a division of Pearson Penguin Canada Inc.)
Penguin Books Ltd., 80 Strand, London WC2R 0RL, England
Penguin Ireland, 25 St. Stephen's Green, Dublin 2, Ireland
(a division of Penguin Books Ltd.)
Penguin Group (Australia), 250 Camberwell Road, Camberwell, Victoria 3124, Australia
(a division of Pearson Australia Group Pty. Ltd.)
Penguin Books India Pvt. Ltd., 11 Community Centre, Panchsheel Park,
New Delhi – 110 017, India
Penguin Group (NZ), 67 Apollo Drive, Rosedale, North Shore 0632, New Zealand
(a division of Pearson New Zealand Ltd.)
Penguin Books (South Africa) (Pty.) Ltd., 24 Sturdee Avenue, Rosebank,
Johannesburg 2196, South Africa

Penguin Books Ltd., Registered Offices: 80 Strand, London WC2R 0RL, England

Published by Plume, a member of Penguin Putnam Inc.
Previously published in a Dutton edition.

First Plume Printing, December, 1999

20 19

REGISTERED TRADEMARK—MARCA REGISTRADA

The Library of Congress has catalogued the Dutton edition as follows:
Rand, Ayn.
Anthem / by Ayn Rand ; with a new introduction and appendix
by Leonard Peikoff. — 50th anniversary ed.
p. cm.
ISBN 978-0-525-94015-9 (hc.)
978-0-452-28125-7 (pbk.)
I. Peikoff, Leonard. II. Title.
PS3535.A547A7 1995
813'.52—dc20 95-9854
CIP

Printed in the United States of America

PUBLISHER'S NOTE
This novel is a work of fiction. Names, characters, places, and incidents either are the product of the author's imagination or are used fictitiously, and any resemblance to actual persons, living or dead, business establishments, event, or locales is entirely coincidental.

INTRODUCTION TO 50TH ANNIVERSARY AMERICAN EDITION

Ayn Rand's working title for this short novel was *Ego*. "I used the word in its exact, literal meaning," she wrote to one correspondent. "I did not mean a symbol of the self—but specifically and actually Man's Self."[1]

Man's self, Ayn Rand held, is his mind or conceptual faculty, the faculty of reason. All man's spiritually distinctive attributes derive from this faculty. For instance, it is reason (man's value judgments) that leads to man's emotions. And it is reason which possesses volition, the ability to make choices.

But reason is a property of the individual. There is no such thing as a collective brain.

The term *ego* combines the above points into a single concept: it designates the mind (and its attributes) considered as an individual possession. The ego, therefore, is that which constitutes the essential identity of a human being. As one dictionary puts it, the ego is "the 'I' or self of any person; [it is] a person as thinking, feeling, and willing, and distinguishing itself from the selves of others and from the objects of its thought."[2]

It is obvious why Ayn Rand exalts man's ego. In doing so, she is (implicitly) upholding the central principles of her philosophy and of her heroes: reason, values, volition, individualism. Her villains, by contrast, do not think, judge, and will; they are second-handers, who allow themselves to be run by others. Having renounced their mind, they are, in a literal sense, self-less.

How does this novella about man's ego, first published in England in 1938, relate to *The Fountainhead* (1943)? *Anthem,* Miss Rand wrote in 1946, is like "the preliminary sketches which artists draw for their future big canvases. I wrote [*Anthem*] while working on *The Fountainhead*—it has the same theme, spirit and intention, although in quite a different form."[3]

One correspondent at the time warned Miss Rand that there are people for whom the word ego is "too strong—even, immoral." She replied: "Why, of course there are. Against whom do you suppose the book was written?"[4]

Although the word ego remains essential to the text, the title was changed to *Anthem* for publication. This was not an attempt to soften the book; it was a step that Ayn Rand took on every novel. Her working titles were invariably blunt and unemotional, naming explicitly, for her own clarity, the central issue of the book; such titles tend to give away to the reader too much too soon and too dryly. Her final titles still pertain to the central issue, but in an indirect and evocative way; they intrigue and even touch the reader while leaving him to discover for himself the book's meaning. (As another example, *The Strike* became in due course *Atlas Shrugged*.)

The present novel, in Miss Rand's mind, was from the outset an ode to man's ego. It was not difficult, therefore, to change the working title: to move from "ego" to "ode" or "anthem," leaving the object celebrated by the ode to be discovered by the reader. "The last two chapters," Miss Rand writes in a letter, "are the actual anthem."[5] The rest is the build-up to it.

There is another reason, I think, for the choice of *anthem* (as against "ode," say, or "celebration"). Anthem is a religiously toned word; its second definition is "a piece of sacred vocal music, usually with words taken from the Scriptures."[6] This does not mean that Ayn Rand conceived her book as religious. The opposite is true.

Ayn Rand explains the point in her Introduction to the Twenty-fifth Anniversary Edition of *The Fountainhead*. Protesting religion's monopoly in the field of ethics, she writes, in part:

> Just as religion has preempted the field of ethics, turning morality *against* man, so it has usurped the highest moral concepts of our language, placing them outside this earth and beyond man's reach. "Exaltation" is usually taken to mean an emotional state evoked by contemplating the supernatural. "Worship" means the emotional experience of loyalty and dedication to something higher than man. "Reverence" means the emotion of a sacred respect, to be experienced on one's knees. "Sacred" means

> superior to and not-to-be-touched-by any concerns of man or of this earth. Etc.
>
> But such concepts do name actual emotions, even though no supernatural dimension exists; and these emotions are experienced as uplifting or ennobling, without the self-abasement required by religious definitions. What, then, is their source or referent in reality? It is the entire emotional realm of man's dedication to a moral ideal. . . .
>
> It is this highest level of man's emotions that has to be redeemed from the murk of mysticism and redirected at its proper object: man.
>
> It is in this sense, with this meaning and intention, that I would identify the sense of life dramatized in *The Fountainhead* as *man-worship*.[7]

For the same reason, Ayn Rand chose the esthetic-moral concept "anthem" for her present title. In doing so, she was not surrendering to mysticism, but waging war against it. She was claiming for man and his ego the *sacred* respect that is actually due not to Heaven, but to life on earth. An "anthem to the ego" is blasphemy to the pious, because it implies that reverence pertains not to God, but to man and, above all, to that fundamental and inherently selfish thing within him that enables him to deal with reality and survive.

There have been plenty of egoists in human history, and there have been plenty of worshipers, too. The egoists were generally cynical "realists" (à la Hobbes), who despised morality; the worshipers, by their own statement, were out of this world. Their clash was an instance of the fact-value dichotomy, which has plagued Western philosophy for many centuries, making facts seem meaningless and values baseless. Ayn Rand's concept of an "anthem to the ego" throws out this vicious dichotomy. Her Objectivist philosophy integrates facts with values—in this instance, the actual nature of man with an exalted and secular admiration for it.

The genre of *Anthem* is determined by its theme. As an anthem, or hymn of praise, the novel is not typical of Ayn Rand in form or in style (although it is typical in content). As Miss Rand has said, *Anthem* has a story, but not a plot, i.e., not a progression of events leading inexorably to an action-climax and a resolution. The closest thing to a climax in *Anthem,* the hero's discovery of the word *I,* is not an existential action, but an internal event, a process of cognition—which is, besides, partly accidental (it is not fully necessitated by the earlier events of the story).[8]

Similarly, *Anthem* does not exemplify Ayn Rand's usual artistic approach, which she called "Romantic Realism." In contrast to her other novels, there is no realistic, contemporary background and relatively little attempt to re-create perceptual, conversational, or psychological detail; the story is set in a remote, primitive future and told in the simple, quasi-biblical terms that befit such a time and world. To Cecil B. De Mille, Ayn Rand described the book as a "dramatic fantasy."[9] To Rose Wilder Lane, in answer to a question, she classified it officially as a "poem."[10]

She held the same view of the book in regard to its adaptation to other media. To Walt Disney, she wrote in 1946 that if a screen version were possible, "I would like to see it done in stylized drawings, rather than with living actors."[11]

Then—in the mid-1960s, as I recall—she received a request from Rudolf Nureyev, who wanted to create a ballet based on *Anthem*. Ordinarily, Miss Rand turned down requests of this kind. But because of the special nature of *Anthem* (and because of her admiration for Nureyev's dancing), she was enthusiastically in favor of his idea. (Unfortunately, neither a movie nor a ballet ever materialized.)

The point is that animation or ballet can capture a fantasy—but not Soviet Russia or the struggles of Roark or the strike of the men of the mind.

Anthem was initially conceived in the early 1920s (or perhaps a bit earlier) as a play. At the time, Ayn Rand was a teenager in Soviet Russia. Some forty years later, she discussed the work's development with an interviewer:

> It was to be a play about a collectivist society of the future in which they lost the word "I." They were all calling each other "we" and it was worked out as much more of a story. There were many characters. It was to be four acts, I think. One of the things I remember about it is that the characters couldn't stand the society. Once in a while, someone would scream and go in-

sane in the middle of one of their collective meetings. The only touch of this left is the people who scream at night.[12]

The play was not specifically anti-*Russian*:

I wasn't taking my revenge on my background. Because if it were that I would have been writing stories laid in Russia or projecting them. It was my intention to wipe out that kind of world totally; I mean I wouldn't want to include Russia or have anything to do with it. My feeling toward Russia at that time was simply an intensified feeling that I've had from childhood and from before the revolutions. I felt that this was so mystical, depraved, rotten a country that I wasn't surprised that they got a Communist ideology—and I felt that one has to get out and find the civilized world.[13]

Ayn Rand got out to the United States in 1926, at the age of twenty-one. But she didn't think of writing *Anthem* here—until she read in the *Saturday Evening Post* a story laid in the future:

It didn't have any particular theme, only the fact that some kind of war had destroyed civilization, and that there is a last survivor in the ruins of New York who rebuilds something. No particular plot. It was just an adventure story, but what interested me was the fact that it was the first time I saw a fantastic story in print—rather than the folks-next-door sort of serials. What impressed me was the fact that they would publish such a story. And so I thought that if they didn't mind fantasy, I would like to try *Anthem*.

I was working on the plot of *The Fountainhead* at that time, which was the worst part of any of my struggles. There was nothing I could do except sit and think—which was miserable. I was doing architectural research, but there was no writing I could do yet, and I had to take time off once in a while to write something. So I wrote *Anthem* that summer of 1937.[14]

What followed was a long struggle to get it published—not a struggle in England, where it was published at once, but in America, where intellectuals, intoxicated by Communism, were at the height (or nadir) of the Red Decade:

> I intended *Anthem* at first as a magazine story or serial . . . but I think my agent said it would not be for the magazines, and she was probably right. Or if she tried them, she didn't succeed. She told me that it should be published as a book, which I hadn't thought of. She submitted it simultaneously to Macmillan in America, who had published *We The Living* and whom I had not left yet, and to the English publisher Cassell. Cassell accepted it immediately; the owner said he was not sure whether it would sell but it was beautiful, and he appreciated it literarily, and he wanted to publish it. Macmillan turned it down; their comment was: the author does not understand socialism.[15]

For the next eight years, nothing was done about *Anthem* in the United States. Then, in 1945, Leonard Read of Pamphleteers, a small conservative outfit in Los Angeles that published nonfiction essays, decided that *Anthem* had to have an American audience; Read brought it out as a pamphlet in 1946. Another conservative house with a meager audience, Caxton, took the book over as a hardcover in 1953. At last, in 1961, about a quarter of a century after it had been written, New American Library issued it as a mass-market paperback.

By such agonizingly drawn-out steps, the country of individualism was finally allowed to discover Ayn Rand's novel of individualism. *Anthem* has now sold nearly 2.5 million copies.

For the first American edition, Ayn Rand rewrote the book. "I have edited [the story] for this publication," she said in her 1946 Foreword, "but have confined the editing to its style. . . . No idea or incident was added or omitted. . . . The story remains as it was. I have lifted its face, but not its spine or spirit; these did not need lifting."[16]

Until her late thirties, when she had mastered English and finished writing *The Fountainhead,* Ayn Rand was not completely satisfied with her command of style. One problem was a degree of overwriting in her earlier work; she was still uncertain at times, she told me once, as to when a point (or an emotion) had been communicated fully and objectively. After 1943, when she was an assured professional both in art and in English, she went back to *Anthem* and (later) to *We The Living,* and revised them in accordance with her mature knowledge.

In editing *Anthem*, she said years later, her main concerns were:

> Precision, clarity, brevity, and eliminating any editorial or slightly purple adjectives. You see, the attempt to have that semi-archaic style was very difficult. Some of the passages were exaggerated. In effect, I was sacrificing content for style—in some places, simply because I didn't know how to say it. By the time I rewrote it after *The Fountainhead,* I was in full control of my style and I knew how to achieve the same effect, but by simple and direct means, without getting too biblical.[17]

For those who want some idea of how in their own work to achieve "precision, clarity, brevity"—and, I might add, beauty, the beauty of a perfect marriage between sound and meaning—I am including as an Appendix to this edition a facsimile of the original British edition of *Anthem,* with Ayn Rand's editorial changes for the American edition written on each page in her own hand. If (ignoring the concrete issue of biblical style) you study her changes and ask "Why?" as you proceed, there is virtually no limit to what you can learn about writing—Ayn Rand's or your own.

Ayn Rand learned a great deal about her art (and about much else, including the applications of her philosophy) during the years of her hard-thinking life. But in essence and as a person, she was immutable. The child who imagined *Anthem* in Russia had the same soul as the woman who edited it nearly thirty years later—and who was still proud of it thirty-five years after that.

A small example of Ayn Rand's constancy can be found in a publicity form she had to fill out for *We The Living* in 1936, a year before she wrote *Anthem*. The form asked authors to state their own philosophy. Her answer, at the age of thirty-one, begins: "To make my life a reason unto itself. I know what I want up to the age of two hundred. Know what you want in life and go after it. I worship *individuals* for their highest possibilities as individuals, and I loathe humanity, for its failure to live up to these possibilities. . . ."[18]

When I come across such characteristic Ayn Rand entries dating as early as 1936 (and even earlier), I think irresistibly of a comment made about Roark by his friend Austen Heller:

> I often think that he's the only one of us who's achieved immortality. I don't mean in the sense of fame and I don't mean he won't die someday. But he's living it. I think he is what the conception really means. You know how people long to be eternal. But they die with every day that passes. . . . They change, they deny, they contradict—and they call it growth. At the end there's nothing left, nothing unreversed or unbetrayed; as if there had never been an entity, only a succession of adjectives fading in and out of an unformed mass. How do they expect a permanence which they have never held for a single moment? But Howard—one can imagine him existing forever.[19]

One can imagine it of Ayn Rand, too. She herself was immortal in the above sense—and she achieved fame, besides. I expect her works, therefore, to live as long as civilization does. Perhaps, like Aristotle's *Logic,* they will even survive another Dark Ages, if and when it comes.

Anthem, in any event, *has* lived—and I am happy to have had the opportunity to introduce its fiftieth anniversary edition in America.

Some of you reading my words will be here to celebrate its hundredth anniversary. As an atheist, I cannot ask you to "keep the faith" in years to come. What I ask instead is: Hold on to reason.

Or, in the style of *Anthem*: Love thine Ego as thyself. Because that's what it is.

—Leonard Peikoff
Irvine, California
October 1994

Notes

1. Letter to Richard de Mille, November, 1946.
2. *Random House Dictionary of the English Language,* College Edition, 1968.
3. Letter to Lorine Pruette, September, 1946.
4. Letter to Richard de Mille, November, 1946.
5. Letter to Lorine Pruette, October, 1946.
6. *Random House Dictionary of the English Language,* College Edition, 1968.
7. Miss Rand's Introduction to 25th Anniversary Edition of *The Fountainhead,* p. ix, paperback.
8. Personal communication.
9. Letter to Cecil B. De Mille, September, 1946.
10. Letter to Rose Wilder Lane, July, 1946.
11. Letter to Walt Disney, September, 1946.
12. Recorded biographical interviews, 1960-61.
13. *Ibid.*
14. *Ibid.*
15. *Ibid.*
16. Forward, 1946 edition of *Anthem,* p.v.
17. Recorded biographical interviews, 1960-61.
18. A Candid Camera of Ayn Rand, June, 1936.
19. *The Fountainhead,* p. 453 paperback.

AUTHOR'S FOREWORD

THIS STORY WAS WRITTEN IN 1937.

I have edited it for this publication, but have confined the editing to its style; I have reworded some passages and cut out some excessive language. No idea or incident was added or omitted; the theme, content and structure are untouched. The story remains as it was. I have lifted its face, but not its spine or spirit; these did not need lifting.

Some of those who read the story when it was first written, told me that I was unfair to the ideals of collectivism; this was not, they said, what collectivism preaches or intends; collectivists do not mean or advocate such things; nobody advocates them.

I shall merely point out that the slogan "Production for use and not for profit" is now accepted by most men as a commonplace, and a commonplace stating a proper, desirable goal. If any intelligible meaning can be discerned in that slogan at all, what is it, if not the idea that the motive of a man's work must be the need of others, not his own need, desire or gain?

Compulsory labor conscription is now practiced or advocated in every country on earth. What is it based on, if not the idea that the state is best qualified to decide where a man can be useful to others, such usefulness being the only consideration, and that his own aims, desires or happiness should be ignored as of no importance?

We have Councils of Vocations, Councils of Eugenics, every possible kind of Council, including a World Council—and if these do not as yet hold total power over us, is it from lack of intention?

"Social gains," "social aims," "social objectives" have become the daily bromides of our language. The necessity of a social justification for all activities and all existence is now taken for granted. There is no proposal outrageous enough but what its author can get a respectful hearing and approbation if he claims that in some undefined way it is for "the common good."

Some might think—though I don't—that nine years ago there was some excuse for men not to see the direction in which the world was going. Today, the evidence is so blatant that no excuse can be claimed by anyone any longer. Those who refuse to see it now are neither blind nor innocent.

The greatest guilt today is that of people who accept collectivism by moral default; the people who seek protection from the necessity of taking a stand, by refusing to admit to themselves the nature of that which they are accepting; the people who support plans specifically designed to achieve serfdom, but hide behind the empty assertion that they are lovers of freedom, with no concrete meaning attached to the word; the people who believe that the content of ideas need not be examined, that principles need not be defined, and that facts can be eliminated by keeping one's eyes shut. They expect, when they find themselves in a world of bloody ruins and concentration camps, to escape moral responsibility by wailing: "But I didn't mean *this!*"

Those who want slavery should have the grace to name it by its proper name. They must face the full meaning of that which they are advocating or condoning; the full, exact, specific meaning of collectivism, of its logical implications, of the principles upon which it is based, and of the ulimate consequences to which these principles will lead.

They must face it, then decide whether this is what they want or not.

—AYN RAND.

April, 1946

I

IT IS A SIN TO WRITE THIS. It is a sin to think words no others think and to put them down upon a paper no others are to see. It is base and evil. It is as if we were speaking alone to no ears but our own. And we know well that there is no transgression blacker than to do or think alone. We have broken the laws. The laws say that men may not write unless the Council of Vocations bid them so. May we be forgiven!

But this is not the only sin upon us. We have committed a greater crime, and for this crime there is no name. What punishment awaits us if it be discovered we know not, for no such crime has come in the memory of men and there are no laws to provide for it.

It is dark here. The flame of the candle stands still in the air. Nothing moves in this tunnel save our hand on the paper. We are alone here under the earth. It is a fearful word, alone. The laws say that none among men may be alone, ever and at any time, for this is the great transgression and the root of all evil. But we have broken many laws. And now there is nothing here save our one body, and it is strange to see only two legs stretched on the ground, and on the wall before us the shadow of our one head.

The walls are cracked and water runs upon them in thin threads without sound, black and glistening as blood. We stole the candle from the larder of the Home of the Street Sweepers. We shall be sentenced to ten years in the Palace of Corrective Detention if it be discovered. But this matters not. It matters only that the light is precious and we should not waste it to write when we need it for that work which is our crime. Nothing matters save the work, our secret, our evil, our precious work. Still, we must also write, for—may the Council have mercy on us!—we wish to speak for once to no ears but our own.

Our name is Equality 7-2521, as it is written on the iron bracelet which all men wear on their left wrists with their names upon it. We are twenty-one years old. We are six feet tall, and this is a burden, for there are not many men who are six feet tall. Ever have the Teachers and the Leaders pointed to us and frowned and said: "There is evil in your bones, Equality 7-2521, for your body has grown beyond the bodies of your brothers." But we cannot change our bones nor our body.

We were born with a curse. It has always driven us to thoughts which are forbidden. It has always given us wishes which men may not wish. We know that we are evil, but there is no will in us and no power to resist it. This is our wonder and our secret fear, that we know and do not resist.

We strive to be like all our brother men, for all men must be alike. Over the portals of the Palace of the World Council, there are words cut in the marble, which we repeat to ourselves whenever we are tempted:

"We are one in all and all in one.
There are no men but only the great WE,
One, indivisible and forever."

We repeat this to ourselves, but it helps us not.

These words were cut long ago. There is green mould in the grooves of the letters and yellow streaks on the marble, which come from more years than men could count. And these words are the truth for they are written on the Palace of the World Council, and the World Council is the body of all truth. Thus has it been ever since the Great Rebirth, and farther back than that no memory can reach.

But we must never speak of the times before the Great Rebirth, else we are sentenced to three years in the Palace of Corrective Detention. It is only the Old Ones who whisper about it in the evenings, in the Home of the Useless. They whisper many strange things, of the towers which rose to the sky, in those Unmentionable Times, and of the wagons which moved without horses, and of the lights which burned without flame. But those times were evil. And those times passed away, when men saw the Great Truth which is this: that all men are one and that there is no will save the will of all men together.

All men are good and wise. It is only we, Equality 7-2521, we alone who were born with a curse. For we are not like our brothers. And as we look back upon our life, we see that it has ever been thus and that it has brought us step by step to our last, supreme transgression, our crime of crimes hidden here under the ground.

We remember the Home of Infants where we lived till we were five years old, together with all the children of the City who had been born in the same year. The sleeping halls there were white and clean and bare of all things save one hundred beds. We were just like all our brothers then, save for the one transgression: we fought with our brothers. There are few offenses blacker than to fight with our brothers, at any age and for any cause whatsoever. The Council of the Home told us so, and of all the children of that year, we were locked in the cellar most often.

When we were five years old, we were sent to the Home of the Students, where there are ten wards, for our ten years of learning. Men must learn till they reach their fifteenth year. Then they go to work. In the Home of the Students we arose when the big bell rang in the tower and we went to our beds when it rang again. Before we removed our garments, we stood in the great sleeping hall, and we raised our right arms, and we said all together with the three Teachers at the head:

"We are nothing. Mankind is all. By the grace of our brothers are we allowed our lives. We exist through, by and for our brothers who are the State. Amen."

Then we slept. The sleeping halls were white and clean and bare of all things save one hundred beds.

We, Equality 7-2521, were not happy in those years in the Home of the Students. It was not that the learning was too hard for us. It was that the learning was too easy. This is a great sin, to be born with a head which is too quick. It is not good to be different from our brothers, but it is evil to be superior to them. The Teachers told us so, and they frowned when they looked upon us.

So we fought against this curse. We tried to forget our lessons, but we always remembered. We tried not to understand what the Teachers taught, but we always understood it before the Teachers had spoken. We looked upon Union 5-3992, who were a pale boy with only half a brain, and we tried to say and do as they did, that we might be like them, like Union 5-3992, but somehow the Teachers knew that we were not. And we were lashed more often than all the other children.

The Teachers were just, for they had been appointed by the Councils, and the Councils are the voice of all justice, for they are the voice of all men. And if sometimes, in the secret darkness of our heart, we regret that which befell us on our fifteenth birthday, we know that it was through our own guilt. We had broken a law, for we had not paid heed to the words of our Teachers. The Teachers had said to us all:

"Dare not choose in your minds the work you would like to do when you leave the Home of the Students. You shall do that which the Council of Vocations shall prescribe for you. For the Council of Vocations knows in its great wisdom where you are needed by your brother men, better than you can know it in your unworthy little minds. And if you are not needed by your brother men, there is no reason for you to burden the earth with your bodies."

We knew this well, in the years of our childhood, but our curse broke our will. We were guilty and we confess it here: we were guilty of the great Transgression of Preference. We preferred some work and some lessons to the others. We did not listen well to the history of all the Councils elected since the Great Rebirth. But we loved the Science of Things. We wished to know. We wished to know about all the things which make the earth around us. We asked so many questions that the Teachers forbade it.

We think that there are mysteries in the sky and under the water and in the plants which grow. But the Council of Scholars has said that there are no mysteries, and the Council of Scholars knows all things. And we learned much from our Teachers. We learned that the earth is flat and that the sun revolves around it, which causes the day and the night. We learned the names of all the winds which blow over the seas and push the sails of our great ships. We learned how to bleed men to cure them of all ailments.

We loved the Science of Things. And in the darkness, in the secret hour, when we awoke in the night and there were no brothers around us, but only their shapes in the beds and their snores, we closed our eyes, and we held our lips shut, and we stopped our breath, that no shudder might let our brothers see or hear or guess, and we thought that we wished to be sent to the Home of the Scholars when our time would come.

All the great modern inventions come from the Home of the Scholars, such as the newest one, which we found only a hundred years ago, of how to make candles from wax and string; also, how to make glass, which is put in our windows to protect us from the rain. To find these things, the Scholars must study the earth and learn from the rivers, from the sands, from the winds and the rocks. And if we went to the Home of the Scholars, we could learn from these also. We could ask questions of these, for they do not forbid questions.

And questions give us no rest. We know not why our curse makes us seek we know not what, ever and ever. But we cannot resist it. It whispers to us that there are great things on this earth of ours, and that we can know them if we try, and that we must know them. We ask, why must we know, but it has no answer to give us. We must know that we may know.

So we wished to be sent to the Home of the Scholars. We wished it so much that our hands trembled under the blankets in the night, and we bit our arm to stop that other pain which we could not endure. It was evil and we dared not face our brothers in the morning. For men may wish nothing for themselves. And we were punished when the Council of Vocations came to give us our life Mandates which tell those who reach their fifteenth year what their work is to be for the rest of their days.

The Council of Vocations came on the first day of spring, and they sat in the great hall. And we who were fifteen and all the Teachers came into the great hall. And the Council of Vocations sat on a high dais, and they had but two words to speak to each of the Students. They called the Students' names, and when the Students stepped before them, one after another, the Council said: "Carpenter" or "Doctor" or "Cook" or "Leader." Then each Student raised their right arm and said: "The will of our brothers be done."

Now if the Council has said 'Carpenter" or "Cook," the Students so assigned go to work and they do not study any further. But if the Council has said "Leader," then those Students go into the Home of the Leaders, which is the greatest house in the City, for it has three stories. And there they study for many years, so that they may become candidates and be elected to the City Council and the State Council and the World Council—by a free and general vote of all men. But we wished not to be a Leader, even though it is a great honor. We wished to be a Scholar.

So we waited our turn in the great hall and then we heard the Council of Vocations call our name: "Equality 7-2521." We walked to the dais, and our legs did not tremble, and we looked up at the Council. There were five members of the Council, three of the male gender and two of the female. Their hair was white and their faces were cracked as the clay of a dry river bed. They were old. They seemed older than the marble of the Temple of the World Council. They sat before us and they did not move. And we saw no breath to stir the folds of their white togas. But we knew that they were alive, for a finger of the hand of the oldest rose, pointed to us, and fell down again. This was the only thing which moved, for the lips of the oldest did not move as they said: "Street Sweeper."

We felt the cords of our neck grow tight as our head rose higher to look upon the faces of the Council, and we were happy. We knew we had been guilty, but now we had a way to atone for it. We would accept our Life Mandate, and we would work for our brothers, gladly and willingly, and we would erase our sin against them, which they did not know, but we knew. So we were happy, and proud of ourselves and of our victory over ourselves. We raised our right arm and we spoke, and our voice was the clearest, the steadiest voice in the hall that day, and we said:

"The will of our brothers be done."

And we looked straight into the eyes of the Council, but their eyes were as cold blue glass buttons.

So we went into the Home of the Street Sweepers. It is a grey house on a narrow street. There is a sundial in its courtyard, by which the Council of the Home can tell the hours of the day and when to ring the bell. When the bell rings, we all arise from our beds. The sky is green and cold in our windows to the east. The shadow on the sundial marks off a half-hour while we dress and eat our breakfast in the dining hall, where there are five long tables with twenty clay plates and twenty clay cups on each table. Then we go to work in the streets of the City, with our brooms and our rakes. In five hours, when the sun is high, we return to the Home and we eat our midday meal, for which one-half hour is allowed. Then we go to work again. In five hours, the shadows are blue on the pavements, and the sky is blue with a deep brightness which is not bright. We come back to have our dinner, which lasts one hour. Then the bell rings and we walk in a straight column to one of the City Halls, for the Social Meeting. Other columns of men arrive from the Homes of the different Trades. The candles are lit, and the Councils of the different Homes stand in a pulpit, and they speak to us of our duties and of our brother men. Then visiting Leaders mount the pulpit and they read to us the speeches which were made in the City Council that day, for the City Council represents all men and all men must know. Then we sing hymns, the Hymn of Brotherhood, and the Hymn of Equality, and the Hymn of the Collective Spirit. The sky is a soggy purple when we return to the Home. Then the bell rings and we walk in a straight column to the City Theatre for three hours of Social Recreation. There a play is shown upon the stage, with two great choruses from the Home of the Actors, which speak and answer all together, in two great voices. The plays are about toil and how good it is. Then we walk back to the Home in a straight column. The sky is like a black sieve pierced by silver drops that tremble, ready to burst through. The moths beat against the street lanterns. We go to our beds and we sleep, till the bell rings again. The sleeping halls are white and clean and bare of all things save one hundred beds.

Thus we lived each day of four years, until two springs ago when our crime happened. Thus must all men live until they are forty. At forty, they are worn out. At forty, they are sent to the Home of the Useless, where the Old Ones live. The Old Ones do not work, for the State takes care of them. They sit in the sun in summer and they sit by the fire in winter. They do not speak often, for they are weary. The Old Ones know that they are soon to die. When a miracle happens and some live to be forty-five, they are the Ancient Ones, and children stare at them when passing by the Home of the Useless. Such is to be our life, as that of all our brothers and of the brothers who came before us.

Such would have been our life, had we not committed our crime which changed all things for us. And it was our curse which drove us to our crime. We had been a good Street Sweeper and like all our brother Street Sweepers, save for our cursed wish to know. We looked too long at the stars at night, and at the trees and the earth. And when we cleaned the yard of the Home of the Scholars, we gathered the glass vials, the pieces of metal, the dried bones which they had discarded. We wished to keep these things to study them, but we had no place to hide them. So we carried them to the City Cesspool. And then we made the discovery.

It was on a day of the spring before last. We Street Sweepers work in brigades of three, and we were with Union 5-3992, they of the half-brain, and with International 4-8818. Now Union 5-3992 are a sickly lad and sometimes they are stricken with convulsions, when their mouth froths and their eyes turn white. But International 4-8818 are different. They are a tall, strong youth and their eyes are like fireflies, for there is laughter in their eyes. We cannot look upon International 4-8818 and not smile in answer. For this they were not liked in the Home of the Students, as it is not proper to smile without reason. And also they were not liked because they took pieces of coal and they drew pictures upon the walls, and they were pictures which made men laugh. But it is only our brothers in the Home of the Artists who are permitted to draw pictures, so International 4-8818 were sent to the Home of the Street Sweepers, like ourselves.

International 4-8818 and we are friends. This is an evil thing to say, for it is a transgression, the great Transgression of Preference, to love any among men better than the others, since we must love all men and all men are our friends. So International 4-8818 and we have never spoken of it. But we know. We know, when we look into each other's eyes. And when we look thus without words, we both know other things also, strange things for which there are no words, and these things frighten us.

So on that day of the spring before last, Union 5-3992 were stricken with convulsions on the edge of the City, near the City Theatre. We left them to lie in the shade of the Theatre tent and we went with International 4-8818 to finish our work. We came together to the great ravine behind the Theatre. It is empty save for trees and weeds. Beyond the ravine there is a plain, and beyond the plain there lies the Uncharted Forest, about which men must not think.

We were gathering the papers and the rags which the wind had blown from the Theatre, when we saw an iron bar among the weeds. It was old and rusted by many rains. We pulled with all our strength, but we could not move it. So we called International 4-8188, and together we scraped the earth around the bar. Of a sudden the earth fell in before us, and we saw an old iron grill over a black hole.

International 4-8818 stepped back. But we pulled at the grill and it gave way. And then we saw iron rings as steps leading down a shaft into a darkness without bottom.

"We shall go down," we said to International 4-8818.

"It is forbidden," they answered.

We said: "The Council does not know of this hole, so it cannot be forbidden."

And they answered: "Since the Council does not know of this hole, there can be no law permitting to enter. And everything which is not permitted by law is forbidden."

But we said: "We shall go, none the less."

They were frightened, but they stood by and watched us go.

We hung on the iron rings with our hands and

our feet. We could see nothing below us. And above us the hole open upon the sky grew smaller and smaller, till it came to be the size of a button. But still we went down. Then our foot touched the ground. We rubbed our eyes, for we could not see. Then our eyes became used to the darkness, but we could not believe what we saw.

No men known to us could have built this place, nor the men known to our brothers who lived before us, and yet it was built by men. It was a great tunnel. Its walls were hard and smooth to the touch; it felt like stone, but it was not stone. On the ground there were long thin tracks of iron, but it was not iron; it felt smooth and cold as glass. We knelt, and we crawled forward, our hand groping along the iron line to see where it would lead. But there was an unbroken night ahead. Only the iron tracks glowed through it, straight and white, calling us to follow. But we could not follow, for we were losing the puddle of light behind us. So we turned and we crawled back, our hand on the iron line. And our heart beat in our fingertips, without reason. And then we knew.

We knew suddenly that this place was left from the Unmentionable Times. So it was true, and those Times had been, and all the wonders of those Times. Hundreds upon hundreds of years ago men knew secrets which we have lost. And we thought: "This is a foul place. They are damned who touch the things of the Unmentionable Times." But our hand which followed the track, as we crawled, clung to the iron as if it would not leave it, as if the skin of our hand were thirsty and begging of the metal some secret fluid beating in its coldness.

We returned to the earth. International 4-8818 looked upon us and stepped back.

"Equality 7-2521," they said, "your face is white."

But we could not speak and we stood looking upon them.

They backed away, as if they dared not touch us. Then they smiled, but it was not a gay smile; it was lost and pleading. But still we could not speak. Then they said:

"We shall report our find to the City Council and both of us will be rewarded."

And then we spoke. Our voice was hard and there was no mercy in our voice. We said:

"We shall not report our find to the City Council. We shall not report it to any men."

They raised their hands to their ears, for never had they heard such words as these.

"International 4-8818," we asked, "will you report us to the Council and see us lashed to death before your eyes?"

They stood straight of a sudden and they answered:

"Rather would we die."

"Then," we said, "keep silent. This place is ours. This place belongs to us, Equality 7-2521, and to no other men on earth. And if ever we surrender it, we shall surrender our life with it also."

Then we saw that the eyes of International 4-8818 were full to the lids with tears they dared not drop. They whispered, and their voice trembled, so that their words lost all shape:

"The will of the Council is above all things, for it is the will of our brothers, which is holy. But if you wish it so, we shall obey you. Rather shall we be evil with you than good with all our brothers. May the Council have mercy upon both our hearts!"

Then we walked away together and back to

the Home of the Street Sweepers. And we walked in silence.

Thus did it come to pass that each night, when the stars are high and the Street Sweepers sit in the City Theatre, we, Equality 7-2521, steal out and run through the darkness to our place. It is easy to leave the Theatre; when the candles are blown and the Actors come onto the stage, no eyes can see us as we crawl under our seat and under the cloth of the tent. Later, it is easy to steal through the shadows and fall in line next to International 4-8818, as the column leaves the Theatre. It is dark in the streets and there are no men about, for no men may walk through the City when they have no mission to walk there. Each night, we run to the ravine, and we remove the stones which we have piled upon the iron grill to hide it from men. Each night, for three hours, we are under the earth, alone.

We have stolen candles from the Home of the Street Sweepers, we have stolen flints and knives and paper, and we have brought them to this place. We have stolen glass vials and powders and acids from the Home of the Scholars. Now we sit in the tunnel for three hours each night and we study. We melt strange metals, and we mix acids, and we cut open the bodies of the animals which we find in the City Cesspool. We have built an oven of the bricks we gathered in the streets. We burn the wood we find in the ravine. The fire flickers in the oven and blue shadows dance upon the walls, and there is no sound of men to disturb us.

We have stolen manuscripts. This is a great offense. Manuscripts are precious, for our brothers in the Home of the Clerks spend one year to copy one single script in their clear handwriting. Manuscripts are rare and they are kept in the Home of the Scholars. So we sit under the earth and we read the stolen scripts. Two years have passed since we found this place. And in these two years we have learned more than we had learned in the ten years of the Home of the Students.

We have learned things which are not in the scripts. We have solved secrets of which the Scholars have no knowledge. We have come to see how great is the unexplored, and many lifetimes will not bring us to the end of our quest. But we wish no end to our quest. We wish nothing, save to be alone and to learn, and to feel as if with each day our sight were growing sharper than the hawk's and clearer than rock crystal.

Strange are the ways of evil. We are false in the faces of our brothers. We are defying the will of our Councils. We alone, of the thousands who walk this earth, we alone in this hour are doing a work which has no purpose save that we wish to do it. The evil of our crime is not for the human mind to probe. The nature of our punishment, if it be discovered, is not for the human heart to ponder. Never, not in the memory of the Ancient Ones' Ancients, never have men done that which we are doing.

And yet there is no shame in us and no regret. We say to ourselves that we are a wretch and a traitor. But we feel no burden upon our spirit and no fear in our heart. And it seems to us that our spirit is clear as a lake troubled by no eyes save those of the sun. And in our heart—strange are the ways of evil!—in our heart there is the first peace we have known in twenty years.

II

LIBERTY 5-3000 . . . LIBERTY five-three thousand . . . Liberty 5-3000. . . .

We wish to write this name. We wish to speak it, but we dare not speak it above a whisper. For men are forbidden to take notice of women, and women are forbidden to take notice of men. But we think of one among women, they whose name is Liberty 5-3000, and we think of no others.

The women who have been assigned to work the soil live in the Home of the Peasants beyond the City. Where the City ends there is a great road winding off to the north, and we Street Sweepers must keep this road clean to the first milepost. There is a hedge along the road, and beyond the hedge lie the fields. The fields are black and ploughed, and they lie like a great fan before us, with their furrows gathered in some hand beyond the sky, spreading forth from that hand, opening wide apart as they come toward us, like black pleats that sparkle with thin, green spangles. Women work in the fields, and their white tunics in the wind are like the wings of sea-gulls beating over the black soil.

And there it was that we saw Liberty 5-3000 walking along the furrows. Their body was straight and thin as a blade of iron. Their eyes were dark and hard and glowing, with no fear in them, no kindness and no guilt. Their hair was golden as the sun; their hair flew in the wind, shining and wild, as if it defied men to restrain it. They threw seeds from their hand as if they deigned to fling a scornful gift, and the earth was as a beggar under their feet.

We stood still; for the first time did we know fear, and then pain. And we stood still that we might not spill this pain more precious than pleasure.

Then we heard a voice from the others call their name: "Liberty 5-3000," and they turned and walked back. Thus we learned their name, and we stood watching them go, till their white tunic was lost in the blue mist.

And the following day, as we came to the northern road, we kept our eyes upon Liberty 5-3000 in the field. And each day thereafter we knew the illness of waiting for our hour on the northern road. And there we looked at Liberty 5-3000 each day. We know not whether they looked at us also, but we think they did.

Then one day they came close to the hedge, and suddenly they turned to us. They turned in a whirl and the movement of their body stopped, as if slashed off, as suddenly as it had started. They stood still as a stone, and they looked straight upon us, straight into our eyes. There was no smile on their face, and no welcome. But their face was taut, and their eyes were dark. Then they turned as swiftly, and they walked away from us.

But the following day, when we came to the road, they smiled. They smiled to us and for us. And we smiled in answer. Their head fell back, and their arms fell, as if their arms and their thin white neck were stricken suddenly with a great lassitude. They were not long looking upon us, but upon the sky. Then they glanced at us over their shoulder, and we felt as if a hand had touched our body, slipping softly from our lips to our feet.

Every morning thereafter, we greeted each other with our eyes. We dared not speak. It is a transgression to speak to men of other Trades, save in groups at the Social Meetings. But once, standing at the hedge, we raised our hand to our forehead and then moved it slowly, palm down, toward Liberty 5-3000. Had the others seen it, they could have guessed nothing, for it looked only as if we were shading our eyes from the sun. But Liberty 5-3000 saw it and understood. They raised their hand to their forehead and moved it as we had. Thus, each day, we greet Liberty 5-3000, and they answer, and no men can suspect.

We do not wonder at this new sin of ours. It is our second Transgression of Preference, for we do not think of all our brothers, as we must, but only of one, and their name is Liberty 5-3000. We do not know why we think of them. We do not know why, when we think of them, we feel of a sudden that the earth is good and that it is not a burden to live.

We do not think of them as Liberty 5-3000 any longer. We have given them a name in our thoughts. We call them the Golden One. But it is a sin to give men names which distinguish them from other men. Yet we call them the Golden One, for they are not like the others. The Golden One are not like the others.

And we take no heed of the law which says that men may not think of women, save at the Time of Mating. This is the time each spring when all the men older than twenty and all the women older than eighteen are sent for one night to the City Palace of Mating. And each of the men have one of the women assigned to them by the Council of Eugenics. Children are born each winter, but women never see their children and children never know their parents. Twice have we been sent to the Palace of Mating, but it is an ugly and shameful matter, of which we do not like to think.

We had broken so many laws, and today we have broken one more. Today, we spoke to the Golden One.

The other women were far off in the field, when we stopped at the hedge by the side of the road. The Golden One were kneeling alone at the moat which runs through the field. And the drops of water falling from their hands, as they raised the water to their lips, were like sparks of fire in the sun. Then the Golden One saw us, and they did not move, kneeling there, looking at us, and circles of light played upon their white tunic, from the sun on the water of the moat, and one sparkling drop fell from a finger of their hand held as frozen in the air.

Then the Golden One rose and walked to the hedge, as if they had heard a command in our eyes. The two other Street Sweepers of our brigade were a hundred paces away down the road. And we thought that International 4-8818 would not betray us, and Union 5-3992 would not understand. So we looked straight upon the Golden One, and we saw the shadows of their lashes on their white cheeks and the sparks of sun on their lips. And we said:

"You are beautiful, Liberty 5-3000."

Their face did not move and they did not avert

their eyes. Only their eyes grew wider, and there was triumph in their eyes, and it was not triumph over us, but over things we could not guess.

Then they asked:

"What is your name?"

"Equality 7-2521," we answered.

"You are not one of our brothers, Equality 7-2521, for we do not wish you to be."

We cannot say what they meant, for there are no words for their meaning, but we know it without words and we knew it then.

"No," we answered, "nor are you one of our sisters."

"If you see us among scores of women, will you look upon us?"

"We shall look upon you, Liberty 5-3000, if we see you among all the women of the earth."

Then they asked:

"Are the Street Sweepers sent to different parts of the City or do they always work in the same places?"

"They always work in the same places," we answered, "and no one will take this road away from us."

"Your eyes," they said, "are not like the eyes of any among men."

And suddenly, without cause for the thought which came to us, we felt cold, cold to our stomach.

"How old are you?" we asked.

They understood our thought, for they lowered their eyes for the first time.

"Seventeen," they whispered.

And we sighed, as if a burden had been taken from us, for we had been thinking without reason of the Palace of Mating. And we thought that we would not let the Golden One be sent to the Palace. How to prevent it, how to bar the will of the Councils, we knew not, but we knew suddenly that we would. Only we do not know why such thought came to us, for these ugly matters bear no relation to us and the Golden One. What relation can they bear?

Still, without reason, as we stood there by the hedge, we felt our lips drawn tight with hatred, a sudden hatred for all our brother men. And the

Golden One saw it and smiled slowly, and there was in their smile the first sadness we had seen in them. We think that in the wisdom of women the Golden One had understood more than we can understand.

Then three of the sisters in the field appeared, coming toward the road, so the Golden One walked away from us. They took the bag of seeds, and they threw the seeds into the furrows of earth as they walked away. But the seeds flew wildly, for the hand of the Golden One was trembling.

Yet as we walked back to the Home of the Street Sweepers, we felt that we wanted to sing, without reason. So we were reprimanded tonight, in the dining hall, for without knowing it we had begun to sing aloud some tune we had never heard. But it is not proper to sing without reason, save at the Social Meetings.

"We are singing because we are happy," we answered the one of the Home Council who reprimanded us.

"Indeed you are happy," they answered. "How else can men be when they live for their brothers?"

And now, sitting here in our tunnel, we wonder about these words. It is forbidden, not to be happy. For, as it has been explained to us, men are free and the earth belongs to them; and all things on earth belong to all men; and the will of all men together is good for all; and so all men must be happy.

Yet as we stand at night in the great hall, removing our garments for sleep, we look upon our brothers and we wonder. The heads of our brothers are bowed. The eyes of our brothers are dull, and never do they look one another in the eyes. The shoulders of our brothers are hunched, and their muscles are drawn, as if their bodies were shrinking and wished to shrink out of sight. And a word steals into our mind, as we look upon our brothers, and that word is fear.

There is fear hanging in the air of the sleeping halls, and in the air of the streets. Fear walks through the City, fear without name, without shape. All men feel it and none dare to speak.

We feel it also, when we are in the Home of the Street Sweepers. But here, in our tunnel, we feel it no longer. The air is pure under the ground. There is no odor of men. And these three hours give us strength for our hours above the ground.

Our body is betraying us, for the Council of the Home looks with suspicion upon us. It is not good to feel too much joy nor to be glad that our body lives. For we matter not and it must not matter to us whether we live or die, which is to be as our brothers will it. But we, Equality 7-2521, are glad to be living. If this is a vice, then we wish no virtue.

Yet our brothers are not like us. All is not well with our brothers. There are Fraternity 2-5503, a quiet boy with wise, kind eyes, who cry suddenly, without reason, in the midst of day or night, and their body shakes with sobs they cannot explain. There are Solidarity 9-6347, who are a bright youth, without fear in the day; but they scream in their sleep, and they scream: "Help us! Help us! Help us!" into the night, in a voice which chills our bones, but the Doctors cannot cure Solidarity 9-6347.

And as we all undress at night, in the dim light of the candles, our brothers are silent, for they dare not speak the thoughts of their minds. For all must agree with all, and they cannot know if their thoughts are the thoughts of all, and so they fear to speak. And they are glad when the candles are blown for the night. But we, Equality 7-2521, look through the window upon the sky, and there is peace in the sky, and cleanliness, and dignity. And beyond the City there lies the plain, and beyond the plain, black upon the black sky, there lies the Uncharted Forest.

We do not wish to look upon the Uncharted

Forest. We do not wish to think of it. But ever do our eyes return to that black patch upon the sky. Men never enter the Uncharted Forest, for there is no power to explore it and no path to lead among its ancient trees which stand as guards of fearful secrets. It is whispered that once or twice in a hundred years, one among the men of the City escape alone and run to the Uncharted Forest, without call or reason. These men do not return. They perish from hunger and from the claws of the wild beasts which roam the Forest. But our Councils say that this is only a legend. We have heard that there are many Uncharted Forests over the land, among the Cities. And it is whispered that they have grown over the ruins of many cities of the Unmentionable Times. The trees have swallowed the ruins, and the bones under the ruins, and all the things which perished.

And as we look upon the Uncharted Forest far in the night, we think of the secrets of the Unmentionable Times. And we wonder how it came to pass that these secrets were lost to the world. We have heard the legends of the great fighting, in which many men fought on one side and only a few on the other. These few were the Evil Ones and they were conquered. Then great fires raged over the land. And in these fires the Evil Ones and all the things made by the Evil Ones were burned. And the fire which is called the Dawn of the Great Rebirth, was the Script Fire where all the scripts of the Evil Ones were burned, and with them all the words of the Evil Ones. Great mountains of flame stood in the squares of the Cities for three months. Then came the Great Rebirth.

The words of the Evil Ones . . . The words of the Unmentionable Times . . . What are the words which we have lost?

May the Council have mercy upon us! We had no wish to write such a question, and we knew not what we were doing till we had written it. We shall not ask this question and we shall not think it. We shall not call death upon our head.

And yet . . . And yet . . .

There is some word, one single word which is not in the language of men, but which had been. And this is the Unspeakable Word, which no men may speak nor hear. But sometimes, and it is rare, sometimes, somewhere, one among men find that word. They find it upon scraps of old manuscripts or cut into the fragments of ancient stones. But when they speak it they are put to death. There is no crime punished by death in this world, save this one crime of speaking the Unspeakable Word.

We have seen one of such men burned alive in the square of the City. And it was a sight which has stayed with us through the years, and it haunts us, and follows us, and it gives us no rest. We were a child then, ten years old. And we stood in the great square with all the children and all the men of the City, sent to behold the burning. They brought the Transgressor out into the square and they led him to the pyre. They had torn out the tongue of the Transgressor, so that they could speak no longer. The Transgressor were young and tall. They had hair of gold and eyes of blue as morning. They walked to the pyre, and their step did not falter. And of all the faces on that square, of all the faces which shrieked and screamed and spat curses upon them, theirs was the calmest and the happiest face.

As the chains were wound over their body at the stake, and a flame set to the pyre, the Transgressor looked upon the City. There was a thin thread of blood running from the corner of their mouth, but the lips were smiling. And a monstrous thought came to us then, which has never left us. We had heard of Saints. There are the Saints of Labor, and the Saints of the Councils, and the Saints of the Great Rebirth. But we had never seen a Saint nor what the likeness of a Saint should be. And we thought then, standing in the square, that the likeliness of a Saint was the face we saw before us in the flames, the face of the Transgressor of the Unspeakable Word.

As the flames rose, a thing happened which no eyes saw but ours, else we would not be living today. Perhaps it had only seemed to us. But it seemed to us that the eyes of the Transgressor had chosen us from the crowd and were looking straight upon us. There was no pain in their eyes and no knowledge of the agony of their body. There was only joy in them, and pride, a pride holier than it is fit for human pride to be. And it seemed as if these eyes were trying to tell us something through the flames, to send into our eyes some word without sound. And it seemed as if these eyes were begging us to gather that word and not to let it go from us and from the earth. But the flames rose and we could not guess the word . . .

What—even if we have to burn for it like the Saint of the pyre—what is the Unspeakable Word?

III

WE, EQUALITY 7-2521, HAVE discovered a new power of nature. And we have discovered it alone, and we are alone to know it.

It is said. Now let us be lashed for it, if we must. The Council of Scholars has said that we all know the things which exist and therefore the things which are not known by all do not exist. But we think that the Council of Scholars is blind. The secrets of this earth are not for all men to see, but only for those who will seek them. We know, for we have found a secret unknown to all our brothers.

We know not what this power is nor whence it comes. But we know its nature, we have watched it and worked with it. We saw it first two years ago. One night, we were cutting open the body of a dead frog when we saw its leg jerking. It was dead, yet it moved. Some power unknown to men was making it move. We could not understand it. Then, after many tests, we found the answer. The frog had been hanging on a wire of copper; and it had been the metal of our knife which had sent a strange power to the copper through the brine of the frog's body. We put a piece of copper and a piece of zinc into a jar of brine, we touched a wire to them, and there, under our fingers, was a miracle which had never occurred before, a new miracle and a new power.

This discovery haunted us. We followed it in preference to all our studies. We worked with it, we tested it in more ways than we can describe, and each step was as another miracle unveiling before us. We came to know that we had found the greatest power on earth. For it defies all the laws known to men. It makes the needle move and turn on the compass which we stole from the Home of the Scholars; but we had been taught, when still a child, that the loadstone points to the north and that this is a law which nothing can change; yet our new power defies all laws. We found that it causes lightning, and never have men known what causes lightning. In thunderstorms, we raised a tall rod of iron by the side of our hole, and we watched it from below. We have seen the lightning strike it again and again. And now we know that metal draws the power of the sky, and that metal can be made to give it forth.

We have built strange things with this discovery of ours. We used for it the copper wires which we found here under the ground. We have walked the length of our tunnel, with a candle lighting the way. We could go no farther than half a mile, for earth and rock had fallen at both ends. But we gathered all the things we found and we brought them to our work place. We found strange boxes with bars of metal inside, with many cords and strands and coils of metal. We found wires that led to strange little globes of glass on the walls; they contained threads of metal thinner than a spider's web.

These things help us in our work. We do not understand them, but we think that the men of the Unmentionable Times had known our power of the sky, and these things had some relation to it. We do not know, but we shall learn. We cannot stop now, even though it frightens us that we are alone in our knowledge.

No single one can possess greater wisdom than the many Scholars who are elected by all men for their wisdom. Yet we can. We do. We have fought against saying it, but now it is said. We do not care. We forget all men, all laws and all things save our metals and our wires. So much is still to be learned! So long a road lies before us, and what care we if we must travel it alone!

IV

MANY DAYS PASSED BEFORE we could speak to the Golden One again. But then came the day when the sky turned white, as if the sun had burst and spread its flame in the air, and the fields lay still without breath, and the dust of the road was white in the glow. So the women of the field were weary, and they tarried over their work, and they were far from the road when we came. But the Golden One stood alone at the hedge, waiting. We stopped and we saw that their eyes, so hard and scornful to the world, were looking at us as if they would obey any word we might speak.

And we said:

"We have given you a name in our thoughts, Liberty 5-3000."

"What is our name?" they asked.

"The Golden One."

"Nor do we call you Equality 7-2521 when we think of you."

"What name have you given us?"

They looked straight into our eyes and they held their head high and they answered:

"The Unconquered."

For a long time we could not speak. Then we said:

"Such thoughts as these are forbidden, Golden One."

"But you think such thoughts as these and you wish us to think them."

We looked into their eyes and we could not lie.

"Yes," we whispered, and they smiled, and then we said: "Our dearest one, do not obey us."

They stepped back, and their eyes were wide and still.

"Speak these words again," they whispered.

"Which words?" we asked. But they did not answer, and we knew it.

"Our dearest one," we whispered.

Never have men said this to women.

The head of the Golden One bowed slowly, and they stood still before us, their arms at their sides, the palms of their hands turned to us, as if their body were delivered in submission to our eyes. And we could not speak.

Then they raised their head, and they spoke simply and gently, as if they wished us to forget some anxiety of their own.

"The day is hot," they said, "and you have worked for many hours and you must be weary."

"No," we answered.

"It is cooler in the fields," they said, "and there is water to drink. Are you thirsty?"

"Yes," we answered, "but we cannot cross the hedge."

"We shall bring the water to you," they said.

Then they knelt by the moat, they gathered water in their two hands, they rose and they held the water out to our lips.

We do not know if we drank that water. We only knew suddenly that their hands were empty, but we were still holding our lips to their hands, and that they knew it, but did not move.

We raised our head and stepped back. For we

did not understand what had made us do this, and we were afraid to understand it.

And the Golden One stepped back, and stood looking upon their hands in wonder. Then the Golden One moved away, even though no others were coming, and they moved stepping back, as if they could not turn from us, their arms bent before them, as if they could not lower their hands.

V

WE MADE IT. WE CREATED IT. We brought it forth from the night of the ages. We alone. Our hands. Our mind. Ours alone and only.

We know not what we are saying. Our head is reeling. We look upon the light which we have made. We shall be forgiven for anything we say tonight. . . .

Tonight, after more days and trials than we can count, we finished building a strange thing, from the remains of the Unmentionable Times, a box of glass, devised to give forth the power of the sky of greater strength than we had ever achieved before. And when we put our wires to this box, when we closed the current—the wire glowed! It came to life, it turned red, and a circle of light lay on the stone before us.

We stood, and we held our head in our hands. We could not conceive of that which we had created. We had touched no flint, made no fire. Yet here was light, light that came from nowhere, light from the heart of metal.

We blew out the candle. Darkness swallowed us. There was nothing left around us, nothing save night and a thin thread of flame in it, as a crack in the wall of a prison. We stretched our hands to the wire, and we saw our fingers in the red glow. We could not see our body nor feel it, and in that moment nothing existed save our two hands over a wire glowing in a black abyss.

Then we thought of the meaning of that which lay before us. We can light our tunnel, and the City, and all the Cities of the world with nothing save metal and wires. We can give our brothers a new light, cleaner and brighter than any they have ever known. The power of the sky can be made to do men's bidding. There are no limits to its secrets and its might, and it can be made to grant us anything if we but choose to ask.

Then we knew what we must do. Our discovery is too great for us to waste our time in sweeping the streets. We must not keep our secret to ourselves, not buried under the ground. We must bring it into the sight of men. We need all our time, we need the work rooms of the Home of the Scholars, we want the help of our brother Scholars and their wisdom joined to ours. There is so much work ahead for all of us, for all the Scholars of the world.

In a month, the World Council of Scholars is to meet in our City. It is a great Council, to which the wisest of all lands are elected, and it meets once a year in the different Cities of the earth. We shall go to this Council and we shall lay before them, as our gift, the glass box with the power of the sky. We shall confess everything to them. They will see, understand and forgive. For our gift is greater than our transgression. They will explain it to the Council of Vocations, and we shall be assigned to the Home of the Scholars. This has never been done before, but neither has a gift such as ours ever been offered to men.

We must wait. We must guard our tunnel as we had never guarded it before. For should any men save the Scholars learn of our secret, they would not understand it, nor would they believe us. They would see nothing, save our crime of working alone, and they would destroy us and our light. We care not about our own body, but our light is . . .

Yes, we do care. For the first time do we care about our body. For this wire is as a part of our body, as a vein torn from us, glowing with our blood. Are we proud of this thread of metal, or of our hands which made it, or is there a line to divide these two?

We stretch out our arms. For the first time do we know how strong our arms are. And a strange thought comes to us: we wonder, for the first time in our life, what we look like. Men never see their own faces and never ask their brothers about it, for it is evil to have concern for their own faces or bodies. But tonight, for a reason we cannot fathom, we wish it were possible to us to know the likeness of our own person.

VI

WE HAVE NOT WRITTEN for thirty days. For thirty days we have not been here, in our tunnel. We had been caught.

It happened on that night when we wrote last. We forgot, that night, to watch the sand in the glass which tells us when three hours have passed and it is time to return to the City Theatre. When we remembered it, the sand had run out.

We hastened to the Theatre. But the big tent stood grey and silent against the sky. The streets of the City lay before us, dark and empty. If we went back to hide in our tunnel, we would be found and our light found with us. So we walked to the Home of the Street Sweepers.

When the Council of the Home questioned us, we looked upon the faces of the Council, but there was no curiosity in those faces, and no anger, and no mercy. So when the oldest of them asked us: "Where have you been?" we thought of our glass box and of our light, and we forgot all else. And we answered:

"We will not tell you."

The oldest did not question us further. They

turned to the two youngest, and said, and their voice was bored:

"Take our brother Equality 7-2521 to the Palace of Corrective Detention. Lash them until they tell."

So we were taken to the Stone Room under the Palace of Corrective Detention. This room has no windows and it is empty save for an iron post. Two men stood by the post, naked but for leather aprons and leather hoods over their faces. Those who had brought us departed, leaving us to the two Judges who stood in a corner of the room. The Judges were small, thin men, grey and bent. They gave the signal to the two strong hooded ones.

They tore our clothes from our body, they threw us down upon our knees and they tied our hands to the iron post.

The first blow of the lash felt as if our spine had been cut in two. The second blow stopped the first, and for a second we felt nothing, then the pain struck us in our throat and fire ran in our lungs without air. But we did not cry out.

The lash whistled like a singing wind. We tried to count the blows, but we lost count. We knew that the blows were falling upon our back. Only we felt nothing upon our back any longer. A flaming grill kept dancing before our eyes, and we thought of nothing save that grill, a grill, a grill of red squares, and then we knew that we were looking at the squares of the iron grill in the door, and there were also the squares of stone on the walls, and the squares which the lash was cutting upon our back, crossing and re-crossing itself in our flesh.

Then we saw a fist before us. It knocked our chin up, and we saw the red froth of our mouth on the withered fingers, and the Judge asked:

"Where have you been?"

But we jerked our head away, hid our face upon our tied hands, and bit our lips.

The lash whistled again. We wondered who was sprinkling burning coal dust upon the floor, for we saw drops of red twinkling on the stones around us.

Then we knew nothing, save two voices snarling steadily, one after the other, even though we knew they were speaking many minutes apart:

"Where have you been where have you been where have you been where have you been? . . ."

And our lips moved, but the sound trickled back into our throat, and the sound was only:

"The light . . . The light . . . The light. . . ."

Then we knew nothing.

We opened our eyes, lying on our stomach on the brick floor of a cell. We looked upon two hands lying far before us on the bricks, and we moved them, and we knew that they were our hands. But we could not move our body. Then we smiled, for we thought of the light and that we had not betrayed it.

We lay in our cell for many days. The door opened twice each day, once for the men who brought us bread and water, and once for the Judges. Many Judges came to our cell, first the humblest and then the most honored Judges of the City. They stood before us in their white togas, and they asked:

"Are you ready to speak?"

But we shook our head, lying before them on the floor. And they departed.

We counted each day and each night as it passed. Then, tonight, we knew that we must escape. For tomorrow the World Council of Scholars is to meet in our City.

It was easy to escape from the Palace of Corrective Detention. The locks are old on the doors and there are no guards about. There is no reason to have guards, for men have never defied the Councils so far as to escape from whatever place they were ordered to be. Our body is healthy and strength returns to it speedily. We lunged against the door and it gave way. We stole through the dark passages, and through dark streets, and down our tunnel.

We lit the candle and we saw that our place had not been found and nothing had been touched. And our glass box stood before us on the cold oven, as we had left it. What matter they now, the scars upon our back!

Tomorrow, in the full light of day, we shall take our box, and leave our tunnel open, and walk through the streets to the Home of the Scholars. We shall put before them the greatest gift ever offered to men. We shall tell them the truth. We shall hand to them, as our confession, these pages we have written. We shall join our hands to theirs, and we shall work together, with the power of the sky, for the glory of mankind. Our blessing upon you, our brothers! Tomorrow, you will take us back into your fold and we shall be an outcast no longer. Tomorrow we shall be one of you again. Tomorrow . . .

VII

IT IS DARK HERE IN THE FOREST. The leaves rustle over our head, black against the last gold of the sky. The moss is soft and warm. We shall sleep on this moss for many nights, till the beasts of the forest come to tear our body. We have no bed now, save the moss, and no future, save the beasts.

We are old now, yet we were young this morning, when we carried our glass box through the streets of the City to the Home of the Scholars. No men stopped us, for there were none about from the Palace of Corrective Detention, and the others knew nothing. No men stopped us at the gate. We walked through empty passages and into the great hall where the World Council of Scholars sat in solemn meeting.

We saw nothing as we entered, save the sky in the great windows, blue and glowing. Then we saw the Scholars who sat around a long table; they were as shapeless clouds huddled at the rise of the great sky. There were men whose famous names we knew, and others from distant lands whose names we had not heard. We saw a great painting on the wall over their heads, of the twenty illustrious men who had invented the candle.

All the heads of the Council turned to us as

we entered. These great and wise of the earth did not know what to think of us, and they looked upon us with wonder and curiosity, as if we were a miracle. It is true that our tunic was torn and stained with brown stains which had been blood. We raised our right arm and we said:

"Our greeting to you, our honored brothers of the World Council of Scholars!"

The Collective 0-0009, the oldest and wisest of the Council, spoke and asked:

"Who are you, our brother? For you do not look like a Scholar."

"Our name is Equality 7-2521," we answered, "and we are a Street Sweeper of this City."

Then it was as if a great wind had stricken the hall, for all the Scholars spoke at once, and they were angry and frightened.

"A Street Sweeper! A Street Sweeper walking in upon the World Council of Scholars! It is not to be believed! It is against all the rules and all the laws!"

But we knew how to stop them.

"Our brothers!" we said. "We matter not, nor

our transgression. It is only our brother men who matter. Give no thought to us, for we are nothing, but listen to our words, for we bring you a gift such as has never been brought to men. Listen to us, for we hold the future of mankind in our hands."

Then they listened.

We placed our glass box upon the table before them. We spoke of it, and of our long quest, and of our tunnel, and of our escape from the Palace of Corrective Detention. Not a hand moved in that hall, as we spoke, nor an eye. Then we put the wires to the box, and they all bent forward and sat still, watching. And we stood still, our eyes upon the wire. And slowly, slowly as a flush of blood, a red flame trembled in the wire. Then the wire glowed.

But terror struck the men of the Council. They leapt to their feet, they ran from the table, and they stood pressed against the wall, huddled together, seeking the warmth of one another's bodies to give them courage.

We looked upon them and we laughed and said:

"Fear nothing, our brothers. There is a great power in these wires, but this power is tamed. It is yours. We give it to you."

Still they would not move.

"We give you the power of the sky!" we cried. "We give you the key to the earth! Take it, and let us be one of you, the humblest among you. Let us all work together, and harness this power, and make it ease the toil of men. Let us throw away our candles and our torches. Let us flood our cities with light. Let us bring a new light to men!"

But they looked upon us, and suddenly we were afraid. For their eyes were still, and small, and evil.

"Our brothers!" we cried. "Have you nothing to say to us?"

Then Collective 0-0009 moved forward. They moved to the table and the others followed.

"Yes," spoke Collective 0-0009, "we have much to say to you."

The sound of their voice brought silence to the hall and to the beat of our heart.

"Yes," said Collective 0-0009, "we have much to say to a wretch who have broken all the laws and who boast of their infamy! How dared you think that your mind held greater wisdom than the minds of your brothers? And if the Councils had decreed that you should be a Street Sweeper, how dared you think that you could be of greater use to men than in sweeping the streets?"

"How dared you, gutter cleaner," spoke Fraternity 9-3452, "to hold yourself as one alone and with the thoughts of the one and not of the many?"

"You shall be burned at the stake," said Democracy 4-6998.

"No," they shall be lashed," said Unanimity 7-3304, "till there is nothing left under the lashes."

"No," said Collective 0-0009, "we cannot decide upon this, our brothers. No such crime has ever been committed, and it is not for us to judge. Nor for any small Council. We shall deliver this creature to the World Council itself and let their will be done."

We looked upon them and we pleaded:

"Our brothers! You are right. Let the will of the Council be done upon our body. We do not care. But the light? What will you do with the light?"

Collective 0-0009 looked upon us, and they smiled.

"So you think that you have found a new power," said Collective 0-0009. "Do all your brothers think that?"

"No," we answered.

"What is not thought by all men cannot be true," said Collective 0-0009.

"You have worked on this alone?" asked International 1-5537.

"Yes," we answered.

"What is not done collectively cannot be good," said International 1-5537.

"Many men in the Homes of the Scholars have had strange new ideas in the past," said Solidarity 8-1164, "but when the majority of their brother Scholars voted against them, they abandoned their ideas, as all men must."

"This box is useless," said Alliance 6-7349.

"Should it be what they claim of it," said Harmony 9-2642, "then it would bring ruin to the Department of Candles. The Candle is a great boon to mankind, as approved by all men. Therefore it cannot be destroyed by the whim of one."

"This would wreck the Plans of the World Council," said Unanimity 2-9913, "and without the Plans of the World Council the sun cannot rise. It took fifty years to secure the approval of all the Councils for the Candle, and to decide upon the number needed, and to re-fit the Plans so as to make candles instead of torches. This touched upon thousands and thousands of men working in scores of States. We cannot alter the Plans again so soon."

"And if this should lighten the toil of men," said Similarity 5-0306, "then it is a great evil, for men have no cause to exist save in toiling for other men."

Then Collective 0-0009 rose and pointed at our box.

"This thing," they said, "must be destroyed."

And all the others cried as one:

"It must be destroyed!"

Then we leapt to the table.

We seized our box, we shoved them aside, and we ran to the window. We turned and we looked at them for the last time, and a rage, such as it is not fit for humans to know, choked our voice in our throat.

"You fools!" we cried. "You fools! You thrice-damned fools!"

We swung our fist through the windowpane, and we leapt out in a ringing rain of glass.

We fell, but we never let the box fall from our hands. Then we ran. We ran blindly, and men and houses streaked past us in a torrent without shape. And the road seemed not to be flat before us, but as if it were leaping up to meet us, and we waited for the earth to rise and strike us in the face. But we ran. We knew not where we were going. We knew only that we must run, run to the end of the world, to the end of our days.

Then we knew suddenly that we were lying on a soft earth and that we had stopped. Trees taller than we had ever seen before stood over us in a great silence. Then we knew. We were in the Uncharted Forest. We had not thought of coming here, but our legs had carried our wisdom, and our legs had brought us to the Uncharted Forest against our will.

Our glass box lay beside us. We crawled to it,

we fell upon it, our face in our arms, and we lay still.

We lay thus for a long time. Then we rose, we took our box and walked on into the forest.

It mattered not where we went. We knew that men would not follow us, for they never enter the Uncharted Forest. We had nothing to fear from them. The forest disposes of its own victims. This gave us no fear either. Only we wished to be away, away from the City and from the air that touches upon the air of the City. So we walked on, our box in our arms, our heart empty.

We are doomed. Whatever days are left to us, we shall spend them alone. And we have heard of the corruption to be found in solitude. We have torn ourselves from the truth which is our brother men, and there is no road back for us, and no redemption.

We know these things, but we do not care. We care for nothing on earth. We are tired.

Only the glass box in our arms is like a living heart that gives us strength. We have lied to ourselves. We have not built this box for the good of our brothers. We built it for its own sake. It is above all our brothers to us, and its truth above their truth. Why wonder about this? We have not many days to live. We are walking to the fangs awaiting us somewhere among the great, silent trees. There is not a thing behind us to regret.

Then a blow of pain struck us, our first and our only. We thought of the Golden One. We thought of the Golden One whom we shall never see again. Then the pain passed. It is best. We are one of the Damned. It is best if the Golden One forget our name and the body which bore that name.

VIII

IT HAS BEEN A DAY OF WONDER, this, our first day in the forest.

We awoke when a ray of sunlight fell across our face. We wanted to leap to our feet, as we have had to leap every morning of our life, but we remembered suddenly that no bell had rung and that there was no bell to ring anywhere. We lay on our back, we threw our arms out, and we looked up at the sky. The leaves had edges of silver that trembled and rippled like a river of green and fire flowing high above us.

We did not wish to move. We thought suddenly that we could lie thus as long as we wished, and we laughed aloud at the thought. We could also rise, or run, or leap, or fall down again. We were thinking that these were thoughts without sense, but before we knew it our body had risen in one leap. Our arms stretched out of their own will, and our body whirled and whirled, till it raised a wind to rustle through the leaves of the bushes. Then our hands seized a branch and swung us high into a tree, with no aim save the wonder of learning the strength of our body. The branch snapped under us and we fell upon the moss that was soft as a cushion. Then our body, losing all sense, rolled over and over on the moss, dry leaves in our tunic, in our hair, in our face. And we heard suddenly that we were laughing, laughing aloud, laughing as if there were no power left in us save laughter.

Then we took our glass box, and we went on into the forest. We went on, cutting through the branches, and it was as if we were swimming through a sea of leaves, with the bushes as waves rising and falling and rising around us, and flinging their green sprays high to the treetops. The trees parted before us, calling us forward. The forest seemed to welcome us. We went on, without thought, without care, with nothing to feel save the song of our body.

We stopped when we felt hunger. We saw birds in the tree branches, and flying from under our footsteps. We picked a stone and we sent it as an arrow at a bird. It fell before us. We made a fire, we cooked the bird, and we ate it, and no meal had ever tasted better to us. And we thought suddenly that there was a great satisfaction to be found in the food which we need and obtain by our own hand. And we wished to be hungry again and soon, that we might know again this strange new pride in eating.

Then we walked on. And we came to a stream which lay as a streak of glass among the trees. It lay so still that we saw no water but only a cut in the earth, in which the trees grew down, upturned, and the sky lay at the bottom. We knelt by the stream and we bent down to drink. And then we stopped. For, upon the blue of the sky below us, we saw our own face for the first time.

We sat still and we held our breath. For our face and our body were beautiful. Our face was not like the faces of our brothers, for we felt no pity when looking upon it. Our body was not like the bodies of our brothers, for our limbs were straight and thin and hard and strong. And we thought that we could trust this being who looked upon us from the stream, and that we had nothing to fear with this being.

We walked on till the sun had set. When the shadows gathered among the trees, we stopped in a hollow between the roots, where we shall sleep tonight. And suddenly, for the first time this day, we remembered that we are the Damned. We remembered it, and we laughed.

We are writing this on the paper we had hidden in our tunic together with the written pages we had brought for the World Council of Scholars, but never given to them. We have much to speak of to ourselves, and we hope we shall find the words for it in the days to come. Now, we cannot speak, for we cannot understand.

IX

We have not written for many days. We did not wish to speak. For we needed no words to remember that which has happened to us.

It was on our second day in the forest that we heard steps behind us. We hid in the bushes, and we waited. The steps came closer. And then we saw the fold of a white tunic among the trees, and a gleam of gold.

We leapt forward, we ran to them, and we stood looking upon the Golden One.

They saw us, and their hands closed into fists, and the fists pulled their arms down, as if they wished their arms to hold them, while their body swayed. And they could not speak.

We dared not come too close to them. We asked, and our voice trembled:

"How come you to be here, Golden One?"

But they whispered only:

"We have found you. . . ."

"How come you to be in the forest?" we asked.

They raised their head, and there was a great pride in their voice; they answered:

"We have followed you."

Then we could not speak, and they said:

"We heard that you had gone to the Uncharted Forest, for the whole City is speaking of it. So on the night of the day when we heard it, we ran away from the Home of the Peasants. We found the marks of your feet across the plain where no men walk. So we followed them, and we went into the forest, and we followed the path where the branches were broken by your body."

Their white tunic was torn, and the branches had cut the skin of their arms, but they spoke as if they had never taken notice of it, nor of weariness, nor of fear.

"We have followed you," they said, "and we shall follow you wherever you go. If danger threatens you, we shall face it also. If it be death, we shall die with you. You are damned, and we wish to share your damnation."

They looked upon us, and their voice was low, but there was bitterness and triumph in their voice:

"Your eyes are as a flame, but our brothers

have neither hope nor fire. Your mouth is cut of granite, but our brothers are soft and humble. Your head is high, but our brothers cringe. You walk, but our brothers crawl. We wish to be damned with you, rather than blessed with all our brothers. Do as you please with us, but do not send us away from you."

Then they knelt, and bowed their golden head before us.

We had never thought of that which we did. We bent to raise the Golden One to their feet, but when we touched them, it was as if madness had stricken us. We seized their body and we pressed our lips to theirs. The Golden One breathed once, and their breath was a moan, and then their arms closed around us.

We stood together for a long time. And we were frightened that we had lived for twenty-one years and had never known what joy is possible to men.

Then we said:

"Our dearest one. Fear nothing of the forest. There is no danger in solitude. We have no need of our brothers. Let us forget their good and our evil, let us forget all things save that we are together and that there is joy as a bond between us.

Give us your hand. Look ahead. It is our own world, Golden One, a strange unknown world, but our own."

Then we walked on into the forest, their hand in ours.

And that night we knew that to hold the body of women in our arms is neither ugly nor shameful, but the one ecstasy granted to the race of men.

We have walked for many days. The forest has no end, and we seek no end. But each day added to the chain of days between us and the City is like an added blessing.

We have made a bow and many arrows. We can kill more birds than we need for our food; we find water and fruit in the forest. At night, we choose a clearing, and we build a ring of fires around it. We sleep in the midst of that ring, and the beasts dare not attack us. We can see their eyes, green and yellow as coals, watching us from the tree branches beyond. The fires smolder as a crown of jewels around us, and smoke stands still in the air, in columns made blue by the moonlight. We sleep together in the midst of the ring, the arms of the Golden One around us, their head upon our breast.

Some day, we shall stop and build a house, when

we shall have gone far enough. But we do not have to hasten. The days before us are without end, like the forest.

We cannot understand this new life which we have found, yet it seems so clear and so simple. When questions come to puzzle us, we walk faster, then turn and forget all things as we watch the Golden One following. The shadows of leaves fall upon their arms, as they spread the branches apart, but their shoulders are in the sun. The skin of their arms is like a blue mist, but their shoulders are white and glowing, as if the light fell not from above, but rose from under their skin. We watch the leaf which has fallen upon their shoulder, and it lies at the curve of their neck, and a drop of dew glistens upon it like a jewel. They approach us, and they stop, laughing, knowing what we think, and they wait obediently, without questions, till it pleases us to turn and go on.

We go on and we bless the earth under our feet. But questions come to us again, as we walk in silence. If that which we have found is the corruption of solitude, then what can men wish for save corruption? If this is the great evil of being alone, then what is good and what is evil?

Everything which comes from the many is good. Everything which comes from one is evil. Thus have we been taught with our first breath. We have broken the law, but we have never doubted it. Yet now, as we walk through the forest, we are learning to doubt.

There is no life for men, save in useful toil for the good of all their brothers. But we lived not, when we toiled for our brothers, we were only weary. There is no joy for men, save the joy shared with all their brothers. But the only things which taught us joy were the power we created in our wires, and the Golden One. And both these joys belong to us alone, they come from us alone, they bear no relation to our brothers, and they do not concern our brothers in any way. Thus do we wonder.

There is some error, one frightful error, in the thinking of men. What is that error? We do not know, but the knowledge struggles within us, struggles to be born.

Today, the Golden One stopped suddenly and said:

"We love you."

But then they frowned and shook their head and looked at us helplessly.

"No," they whispered, "that is not what we wished to say."

They were silent, then they spoke slowly, and their words were halting, like the words of a child learning to speak for the first time:

"We are one . . . alone . . . and only . . . and we love you who are one . . . alone . . . and only."

We looked into each other's eyes and we knew that the breath of a miracle had touched us, and fled, and left us groping vainly.

And we felt torn, torn for some word we could not find.

X

WE ARE SITTING AT A TABLE and we are writing this upon paper made thousands of years ago. The light is dim, and we cannot see the Golden One, only one lock of gold on the pillow of an ancient bed. This is our home.

We came upon it today, at sunrise. For many days we had been crossing a chain of mountains. The forest rose among the cliffs, and whenever we walked out upon a barren stretch of rock we saw great peaks before us in the west, and to the north of us, and to the south, as far as our eyes could see. The peaks were red and brown, with the green streaks of forests as veins upon them, with blue mists as veils over their heads. We had never heard of these mountains, nor seen them marked on any map. The Uncharted Forest has protected them from the Cities and from the men of the Cities.

We climbed paths where the wild goat dared not follow. Stones rolled from under our feet, and we heard them striking the rocks below, farther and farther down, and the mountains rang with each stroke, and long after the strokes had died. But we went on, for we knew that no men would ever follow our track nor reach us here.

Then today, at sunrise, we saw a white flame

among the trees, high on a sheer peak before us. We thought that it was a fire and we stopped. But the flame was unmoving, yet blinding as liquid metal. So we climbed toward it through the rocks. And there, before us, on a broad summit, with the mountains rising behind it, stood a house such as we had never seen, and the white fire came from the sun on the glass of its windows.

The house had two stories and a strange roof flat as a floor. There was more window than wall upon its walls, and the windows went on straight around the corners, though how this kept the house standing we could not guess. The walls were hard and smooth, of that stone unlike stone which we had seen in our tunnel.

We both knew it without words: this house was left from the Unmentionable Times. The trees had protected it from time and weather, and from men who have less pity than time and weather. We turned to the Golden One and we asked:

"Are you afraid?"

But they shook their head. So we walked to the door, and we threw it open, and we stepped together into the house of the Unmentionable Times.

We shall need the days and the years ahead, to

look, to learn and to understand the things of this house. Today, we could only look and try to believe the sight of our eyes. We pulled the heavy curtains from the windows and we saw that the rooms were small, and we thought that not more than twelve men could have lived here. We thought it was strange that men had been permitted to build a house for only twelve.

Never had we seen rooms so full of light. The sunrays danced upon colors, colors, more colors than we thought possible, we who had seen no houses save the white ones, the brown ones and the grey. There were great pieces of glass on the walls, but it was not glass, for when we looked upon it we saw our own bodies and all the things behind us, as on the face of a lake. There were strange things which we had never seen and the use of which we do not know. And there were globes of glass everywhere, in each room, the globes with the metal cobwebs inside, such as we had seen in our tunnel.

We found the sleeping hall and we stood in awe upon its threshold. For it was a small room and there were only two beds in it. We found no other beds in the house, and then we knew that only two had lived here, and this passes understanding. What kind of world did they have, the men of the Unmentionable Times?

We found garments, and the Golden One gasped at the sight of them. For they were not white tunics, nor white togas; they were of all colors, no two of them alike. Some crumbled to dust as we touched them. But others were of heavier cloth, and they felt soft and new in our fingers.

We found a room with walls made of shelves, which held rows of manuscripts, from the floor to the ceiling. Never had we seen such a number of them, nor of such strange shape. They were not soft and rolled, they had hard shells of cloth and leather; and the letters on their pages were so small and so even that we wondered at the men who had such handwriting. We glanced through the pages, and we saw that they were written in our language, but we found many words which we could not understand. Tomorrow, we shall begin to read these scripts.

When we had seen all the rooms of the house, we looked at the Golden One and we both knew the thought in our minds.

"We shall never leave this house," we said, "nor let it be taken from us. This is our home and the end of our journey. This is your house, Golden One, and ours, and it belongs to no other men whatever as far as the earth may stretch. We shall not share it with others, as we share not our joy with them, nor our love, nor our hunger. So be it to the end of our days."

"Your will be done," they said.

Then we went out to gather wood for the great hearth of our home. We brought water from the stream which runs among the trees under our windows. We killed a mountain goat, and we brought its flesh to be cooked in a strange copper pot we found in a place of wonders, which must have been the cooking room of the house.

We did this work alone, for no words of ours could take the Golden One away from the big glass which is not glass. They stood before it and they looked and looked upon their own body.

When the sun sank beyond the mountains, the Golden One fell asleep on the floor, amidst jewels, and bottles of crystal, and flowers of silk. We lifted the Golden One in our arms and we carried them to a bed, their head falling softly upon our shoulder. Then we lit a candle, and we brought paper from the room of the manuscripts, and we sat by the window, for we knew that we could not sleep tonight.

And now we look upon the earth and sky. This spread of naked rock and peaks and moonlight is like a world ready to be born, a world that waits.

It seems to us it asks a sign from us, a spark, a first commandment. We cannot know what word we are to give, nor what great deed this earth expects to witness. We know it waits. It seems to say it has great gifts to lay before us, but it wishes a greater gift from us. We are to speak. We are to give its goal, its highest meaning to all this glowing space of rock and sky.

We look ahead, we beg our heart for guidance in answering this call no voice has spoken, yet we have heard. We look upon our hands. We see the dust of centuries, the dust which hid great secrets and perhaps great evils. And yet it stirs no fear within our heart, but only silent reverence and pity.

May knowledge come to us! What is the secret our heart has understood and yet will not reveal to us, although it seems to beat as if it were endeavoring to tell it?

XI

I AM. I THINK. I WILL.

My hands . . . My spirit . . . My sky . . . My forest . . . This earth of mine. . . .

What must I say besides? These are the words. This is the answer.

I stand here on the summit of the mountain. I lift my head and I spread my arms. This, my body and spirit, this is the end of the quest. I wished to know the meaning of things. I am the meaning. I wished to find a warrant for being. I need no warrant for being, and no word of sanction upon my being. I am the warrant and the sanction.

It is my eyes which see, and the sight of my eyes grants beauty to the earth. It is my ears which hear, and the hearing of my ears gives its song to the world. It is my mind which thinks, and the judgment of my mind is the only searchlight that can find the truth. It is my will which chooses, and the choice of my will is the only edict I must respect.

Many words have been granted me, and some

are wise, and some are false, but only three are holy: "I will it!"

Whatever road I take, the guiding star is within me; the guiding star and the loadstone which point the way. They point in but one direction. They point to me.

I know not if this earth on which I stand is the core of the universe or if it is but a speck of dust lost in eternity. I know not and I care not. For I know what happiness is possible to me on earth. And my happiness needs no higher aim to vindicate it. My happiness is not the means to any end. It is the end. It is its own goal. It is its own purpose.

Neither am I the means to any end others may wish to accomplish. I am not a tool for their use. I am not a servant of their needs. I am not a bandage for their wounds. I am not a sacrifice on their altars.

I am a man. This miracle of me is mine to own and keep, and mine to guard, and mine to use, and mine to kneel before!

I do not surrender my treasures, nor do I share them. The fortune of my spirit is not to be blown into coins of brass and flung to the winds as alms for the poor of the spirit. I guard my treasures:

my thought, my will, my freedom. And the greatest of these is freedom.

I owe nothing to my brothers, nor do I gather debts from them. I ask none to live for me, nor do I live for any others. I covet no man's soul, nor is my soul theirs to covet.

I am neither foe nor friend to my brothers, but such as each of them shall deserve of me. And to earn my love, my brothers must do more than to have been born. I do not grant my love without reason, nor to any chance passer-by who may wish to claim it. I honor men with my love. But honor is a thing to be earned.

I shall choose my friends among men, but neither slaves nor masters. And I shall choose only such as please me, and them I shall love and respect, but neither command nor obey. And we shall join our hands when we wish, or walk alone when we so desire. For in the temple of his spirit, each man is alone. Let each man keep his temple untouched and undefiled. Then let him join hands with others if he wishes, but only beyond his holy threshold.

For the word "We" must never be spoken, save by one's choice and as a second thought. This word must never be placed first within man's soul, else it becomes a monster, the root of all the evils on earth, the root of man's torture by men, and of an unspeakable lie.

The word "We" is as lime poured over men, which sets and hardens to stone, and crushes all beneath it, and that which is white and that which is black are lost equally in the grey of it. It is the word by which the depraved steal the virtue of the good, by which the weak steal the might of the strong, by which the fools steal the wisdom of the sages.

What is my joy if all hands, even the unclean, can reach into it? What is my wisdom, if even the fools can dictate to me? What is my freedom, if all creatures, even the botched and the impotent, are my masters? What is my life, if I am but to bow, to agree and to obey?

But I am done with this creed of corruption.

I am done with the monster of "We," the word of serfdom, of plunder, of misery, falsehood and shame.

And now I see the face of god, and I raise this god over the earth, this god whom men have sought since men came into being, this god who will grant them joy and peace and pride.

This god, this one word:

"I."

XII

IT WAS WHEN I READ the first of the books I found in my house that I saw the word "I." And when I understood this word, the book fell from my hands, and I wept, I who had never known tears. I wept in deliverance and in pity for all mankind.

I understood the blessed thing which I had called my curse. I understood why the best in me had been my sins and my transgressions; and why I had never felt guilt in my sins. I understood that centuries of chains and lashes will not kill the spirit of man nor the sense of truth within him.

I read many books for many days. Then I called the Golden One, and I told her what I had read and what I had learned. She looked at me and the first words she spoke were:

"I love you."

Then I said:

"My dearest one, it is not proper for men to be without names. There was a time when each man had a name of his own to distinguish him from all other men. So let us choose our names. I have read of a man who lived many thousands of years ago, and of all the names in these books, his is the one I wish to bear. He took the light of the gods and he brought it to men, and he taught men to be gods. And he suffered for his deed as all bearers of light must suffer. His name was Prometheus."

"It shall be your name," said the Golden One.

"And I have read of a goddess," I said, "who was the mother of the earth and of all the gods. Her name was Gaea. Let this be your name, my Golden One, for you are to be the mother of a new kind of gods."

"It shall be my name," said the Golden One.

Now I look ahead. My future is clear before me. The Saint of the pyre had seen the future when he chose me as his heir, as the heir of all the saints and all the martyrs who came before him and who died for the same cause, for the same word, no matter what name they gave to their cause and their truth.

I shall live here, in my own house. I shall take my food from the earth by the toil of my own hands. I shall learn many secrets from my books. Through the years ahead, I shall rebuild the achievements of the past, and open the way to carry them further, the achievements which are open to me, but closed forever to my brothers, for their minds are shackled to the weakest and dullest ones among them.

I have learned that my power of the sky was known to men long ago; they called it Electricity. It was the power that moved their greatest inventions. It lit this house with light which came from those globes of glass on the walls. I have found the engine which produced this light. I shall learn how to repair it and how to make it work again. I shall learn how to use the wires which carry this power. Then I shall build a barrier of wires around my home, and across the paths which lead to my home; a barrier light as a cobweb, more impassable then a wall of granite; a barrier my brothers will never be able to cross. For they have nothing to fight me with, save the brute forces of their numbers. I have my mind.

Then here, on this mountaintop, with the world below me and nothing above me but the sun, I shall live my own truth. Gaea is pregnant with my child. Our son will be raised as a man. He will be taught to say "I" and to bear the pride of it. He will be taught to walk straight and on his own feet. He will be taught reverence for his own spirit.

When I shall have read all the books and learned my new way, when my home will be ready and my earth tilled, I shall steal one day, for the last time, into the cursed City of my birth. I shall call to me my friend who has no name save International 4-8818, and all those like him, Fraternity 2-5503, who cries without reason, and Solidarity 9-6347 who calls for help in the night, and a few others. I shall call to me all the men and the women whose spirit has not been killed within them and who suffer under the yoke of their brothers. They will follow me and I shall lead them to my fortress. And here, in this uncharted wilderness, I and they, my chosen friends, my fellow-builders, shall write the first chapter in the new history of man.

These are the things before me. And as I stand here at the door of glory, I look behind me for the last time. I look upon the history of men, which I have learned from the books, and I wonder. It was a long story, and the spirit which moved it was the spirit of man's freedom. But what is freedom? Freedom from what? There is nothing to take a man's freedom away from him, save other men. To be free, a man must be free of his brothers. That is freedom. This and nothing else.

At first, man was enslaved by the gods. But he broke their chains. Then he was enslaved by the kings. But he broke their chains. He was enslaved by his birth, by his kin, by his race. But he broke their chains. He declared to all his brothers that a man has rights which neither god nor king nor other men can take away from him, no matter what their number, for his is the right of man, and there is no right on earth above this right. And he stood on the threshold of the freedom for which the blood of the centuries behind him had been spilled.

But then he gave up all he had won, and fell lower than his savage beginning.

What brought it to pass? What disaster took their reason away from men? What whip lashed them to their knees in shame and submission? The worship of the word "We."

When men accepted that worship, the structure of centuries collapsed about them, the structure whose every beam had come from the thought of some one man, each in his day down the ages, from the depth of some one spirit, such spirit as existed but for its own sake. Those men who survived—those eager to obey, eager to live for one another, since they had nothing else to vindicate them—those men could neither carry on, nor preserve what they had received. Thus did all thought, all science, all wisdom perish on earth. Thus did men—men with nothing to offer save their great number—lose the steel towers, the flying ships, the power wires, all the things they had not created and could never keep. Perhaps, later, some men had been born with the mind and the courage to recover these things which were lost; perhaps these men came before the Councils of Scholars. They were answered as I have been answered—and for the same reasons.

But I still wonder how it was possible, in those graceless years of transition, long ago, that men did not see whither they were going, and went on, in blindness and cowardice, to their fate. I wonder, for it is hard for me to conceive how men who knew the word "I," could give it up and not know what they lost. But such has been the story, for I have lived in the City of the damned, and I know what horror men permitted to be brought upon them.

Perhaps, in those days, there were a few among men, a few of clear sight and clean soul, who refused to surrender that word. What agony must have been theirs before that which they saw coming and could not stop! Perhaps they cried out in protest and in warning. But men paid no heed to their warning. And they, these few, fought a hopeless battle, and they perished with their banners smeared by their own blood. And they chose to perish, for they knew. To them, I send my salute across the centuries, and my pity.

Theirs is the banner in my hand. And I wish I had the power to tell them that the despair of their hearts was not to be final, and their night was not without hope. For the battle they lost can never be lost. For that which they died to save can never perish. Through all the darkness, through all the shame of which men are capable, the spirit of man will remain alive on this earth. It may sleep, but it will awaken. It may wear chains, but it will break through. And man will go on. Man, not men.

Here, on this mountain, I and my sons and my chosen friends shall build our new land and our fort. And it will become as the heart of the earth, lost and hidden at first, but beating, beating louder each day. And word of it will reach every corner of the earth. And the roads of the world will become as veins which will carry the best of the world's blood to my threshold. And all my brothers, and the Councils of my brothers, will hear of it, but they will be impotent against me. And the day will come when I shall break all the chains of the earth, and raze the cities of the enslaved, and my home will become the capital of a world where each man will be free to exist for his own sake.

For the coming of that day shall I fight, I and my sons and my chosen friends. For the freedom of Man. For his rights. For his life. For his honor.

And here, over the portals of my fort, I shall cut in the stone the word which is to be my beacon and my banner. The word which will not die, should we all perish in battle. The word which can never die on this earth, for it is the heart of it and the meaning and the glory.

The sacred word:

EGO

Anthem was originally published in England in 1938. For its first American edition, in 1946, Ayn Rand rewrote the book. Her purpose, she said years later, was "precision, clarity, brevity, and eliminating any editorial or slightly purple adjectives." For those interested in Ayn Rand's literary development, there follows a facsimile of the original English edition, with Ayn Rand's editorial changes for the American edition written on each page in her own hand.

ANTHEM

by

AYN RAND

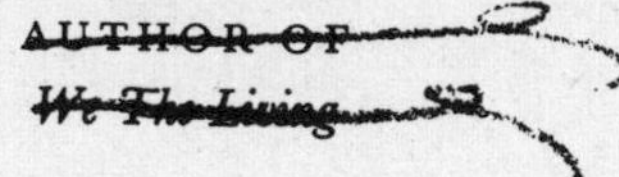

~~AUTHOR OF~~

~~*We The Living*~~

CASSELL
AND COMPANY, LIMITED
LONDON, TORONTO, MELBOURNE
~~AND~~ SYDNEY

First Published 1938

PRINTED AT
THE BROADWATER PRESS
WELWYN : HERTFORDSHIRE
F. 338

ANTHEM

~~CHAPTER~~ I

It is a sin to write this. It is a sin to think words no others think and to put them down upon a paper no others are to see. It is base and evil. It is as if we were speaking alone to no ears but our own. And we know well that there is no transgression blacker than to do or think alone. We have broken the laws. The laws say that men may not write unless the Council of Vocations bid them so. May we be forgiven!

But this is not the only sin upon us. ~~Our sins are like stars in the sky which are without number.~~ We have committed a greater crime, and for this crime there is no name. What punishment awaits us if it be discovered we know not, for no such crime has come in the memory of men and there are no laws to provide for it.

It is dark here. The flame of the candle stands still in the air. Nothing moves in this tunnel save our hand on the paper. We are alone here under the earth. It is a fearful word, alone. The laws say that none among men may be alone, ever and at any time, for this is the great transgression and the root of all evil. But we have broken many laws. And now there is nothing here save our one body, and it is strange to see only two legs stretched in the mud, and on the wall before us the shadow of our one head.

The walls are cracked and water runs upon them in thin threads without sound, black and glistening as blood. We stole the candle from the larder of the Home of the

Street Sweepers. We shall be sentenced to ten years in the Palace of Corrective Detention if it be discovered. But this matters not. It matters only that the light is precious and we should not waste it to write when we need it for that work which is our crime. Nothing matters save the work, our secret, our evil, our precious work. Still, we must also write, for—may the Council have mercy upon us!—we wish to speak for once to no ears but our own.

Our name is Equality 7-2521, as it is written upon the iron bracelet which all men wear on their left wrists with their names upon it. We are twenty-one years old. We are six feet one inch tall, and this is a burden, for there are not many men who are six feet one inch tall. Ever have the Teachers and the Leaders pointed to us and frowned and said: "There is evil in your bones, Equality 7-2521, for your body has grown beyond the bodies of your brothers." We

~~are ashamed of~~ our bones ~~and of the things inside~~ our body ~~but we cannot change them~~.

We were born with a curse. ~~Ever has~~ It driven us to thoughts which are forbidden. ~~Ever has~~ It given us wishes which men may not wish. We know that we are evil, but there is no will in us and no power to resist it. This is our wonder and our secret fear, that we know and do not resist.

We strive to be like all our brother men, for all men must be alike. Over the portals of the Palace of the World Council, ~~there is a great piece of marble, and~~ there are words cut in the marble, which we repeat to ourselves whenever we are tempted:

"We are one in all and all in one.
There are no men but only the great
WE, one, indivisible and forever."

We repeat this to ourselves, but it helps us not.

These words were cut long ago. There is green ~~moss~~ in the grooves of the letters and yellow streaks upon the marble pieces which come from more years than men could count. And these words are the truth, for they are written on the Palace of the World Council, and the World Council is the body of all truth. Thus has it been ever since the Great Re-birth, and farther back than that no memory can reach. It is said that before the Great Re-birth men were blind and ignorant as beasts, for they had to seek the truth. This is strange and fearful to us, for our age has found it. But we must never speak of the times before the Great Re-birth, else we are sentenced to three years in the Palace of Corrective Detention. It is only the Old Ones who whisper about it in the evenings, in the Home of the Useless. They whisper many things, strange and inconceivable, of the towers which rose to the sky, in those Unmentionable Times, and of the wagons which moved without horses, and of the lights which burned without flame. But those times were ~~ruled by evils of which we dare not think.~~ And those times passed away, when men saw the Great Truth which is this: that all men are one and that there is no will save the will of all men together.

All men are good and wise. It is only we, Equality 7-2521, we alone who were born with a curse. For we are not ~~[illegible] such thing is not to be spoken, but only whispered in [illegible]~~ like our brothers. And as we look back upon our life, we see that it has ever been thus and that it has brought us step by step to our last, supreme transgression, our crime of crimes hidden here under the ground.

We remember the Home of the Infants where we lived till we were five years old, together with all the children of the City who had been born in the same year. The sleeping halls there were white and clean and bare of all things save one hundred beds. We were just like all our brothers then, save for the one transgression: we fought with our brothers. There are few offences blacker than to fight with our brothers, at any age and for any cause whatsoever. The Council of the Home told us so, and of all the children of that year, we were ~~most often~~ locked in the ~~Dark Place, to sit for two days naked on the stone flooring~~ cellar most often.

When we were five years old we were sent to the Home of the Students, where there are ten wards, for our ten years of learning. Men must learn till they reach their fifteenth year. Then they go to work. In the Home of the Students we arose when the big bell rang in the tower and we went to our beds when it rang again. Before we removed our garments, we stood in the great sleeping hall, and we raised our right arms, and we said all together with the three Teachers at the head ~~of the hall~~:

"We are nothing. Mankind is all. By the

grace of our brothers are we allowed our lives. We exist through, by and for our brothers which are the State. Amen."

Then we slept. The sleeping halls were white and clean and bare of all things save one hundred beds.

We, Equality 7-2521, were not happy in those years in the Home of the Students. It was not that the learning was too hard for us. It was that the learning was too easy. This is a great sin, to be born with a head which is too quick. It is not good to be different from our brothers, but it is evil to be superior to them. The Teachers told us so, and they frowned when they looked upon us.

So we fought against this curse. We tried to forget our lessons, but we always remembered. We tried not to understand what the Teachers taught, but we always understood it before the Teachers had spoken. We looked upon Union 5-3992, who were a pale boy with only half a brain, and we tried to say and do as they did, that we might be like them, like Union 5-3992, but somehow the Teachers knew that we were not. And we were lashed more often than all the other children.

The Teachers were just, for they had been appointed by the Councils, and the Councils are the voice of all justice, for they are the voice of all men. ~~The world of men is but kindness and love~~. And if sometimes, in the secret darkness of our heart, we regret that which befell us on our fifteenth birthday, we know that it was through our own guilt. We had broken a law, for we had not paid heed to the words of our Teachers. The Teachers had said ~~unto~~ to us all:

"Dare not choose in your minds the work you would like to do when you leave the Home of the Students. You shall do that which the Council of Vocations shall prescribe for you. For the Council of Vocations knows in its great wisdom where you are needed by your brother men, better than you can know it in your unworthy little minds. And if you are not needed by your brother men, there is no reason for you to burden the earth with your bodies."

This is just, for the Councils have a great duty to carry, and they who have the duty must also have the power. It is the Councils who hold the reins of the world, who feed us all and clothe us and shelter us in our sleep. None among men go hungry, nor do they tremble, homeless, in the autumn rains —upon this wonderful earth of ours. Down the roads of the world heavy carts stream day and night, carrying men's sustenance to men; fields of wheat ripen in the sun; wheels turn, and axes bite into forests, and picks split the granite of the earth—and each blow, each tensed muscle, each trembling green blade of wheat is under the great wisdom of our fathers' hand, our fathers who are the Councils; these Councils who bend

14

their sage, tireless heads in the candle light over miles and mountains of maps, that each morsel of food may find its way on time to the humblest stomach. But to do this, our Councils hold the power to command their life work unto each among men. Else what order would there be upon earth?

We knew this well, in the years of our childhood, but our curse was upon us and it gave us no rest. We were guilty and we confess it here: we were guilty of the great Transgression of Preference. We preferred some work and some lessons to the others. We did not listen well to the history of all the Councils elected since the Great Re-birth. But we loved the Science of Things. We wished to know. We wished to know about all the things which make the earth around us. We asked so many questions that the Teachers forbade it. We think that there are mysteries in the sky and under the water and in the plants which grow. But the Council of Scholars has said that there are no mysteries, and the Council of Scholars knows all things. And we learned much from our Teachers. We learned that the earth is flat and that the sun revolves around it, which causes the day and the night. We learned the names of all the winds which blow over the seas and push the sails of our great ships. We learned how to bleed men to cure them of all ailments.

~~So~~ we loved the Science of ~~the Earth~~. And in the darkness, in the secret hour, when we awoke in the night and there were no brothers around us, but only their ~~white~~ shapes in the beds and their snores, we closed our eyes, and we held our lips shut ~~as a trap,~~ and we ~~breathed not~~, that no shudder might let our brothers see or hear or guess, and we thought that we wished to be ~~assigned~~ to the Home of the Scholars when our time would come. All the great modern inventions come from the Home of the Scholars, such as the newest one, which was found only a hundred years ago, of how to make candles from wax and string, ~~which give us light~~; also, how to make ~~this new thing called~~ glass, which is put in our windows to protect us from the rain. ~~And~~ to find these things, the Scholars must study the earth and learn from the rivers, from the sands, from the winds and the rocks. And if we went to the Home of the Scholars, we could learn from these also. We could ask questions of these, for they do not forbid questions.

And questions give us no rest. We know not ~~what demons sit inside our skull and~~ make us seek we know not what, ever and ever. But we cannot resist ~~them. They~~ whisper to us that there are things ~~un-dreamed~~ on this earth of ours, and that we can know them if we ~~but~~ try, and that we must know them. We ask ~~the demons~~ why must we know, but they have no answer to give. We must know that we may know. We cannot understand this evil wish of ours, but neither can we conquer it. So we longed to be sent to the Home of the Scholars. We longed for it so much that our fingers shook under the blankets in the night, and something hurt us in our chest, and we bit our arm to stop that other pain which we could not endure. It was evil and we dared not face our brothers in the morning. For men may wish nothing for themselves. And we were punished when the Council of Vocations came to give us our Life Mandates which tell those who reach their fifteenth year what their work is to be for the rest of their days.

The Council of Vocations came on the first day of spring, and they sat in the great hall. And we who were fifteen and all the Teachers came into the great hall. And the Council of Vocations sat on a high dais, and they had but two words to speak to each of the Students. They called the Students' names, and when the Students stepped before them, one after another, the Council said: "Carpenter" or "Doctor" or "Cook" or "Leader." Then each Student raised their right arm and said: "The will of our brothers be done."

Now if the Council has said "Carpenter" or "Cook," the Students so assigned go ~~forth~~ to work and they do not study any further. But if the Council has said "Leader," then those Students go ~~forth~~ into the Home of the Leaders, which is the greatest house in the City, for it has three stories. And there they ~~learn many things~~ for many years, so that they may become candidates and be elected to the City Council and the State Council and the World Council—by a free and general vote of all men. But we wished not to be a Leader, even though it is a great honour. We wished to be a Scholar.

~~and the pain of our wish hurt us in our body~~.

So we awaited our turn in the great hall and then we heard the Council of Vocations call our name: "Equality 7-2521." We walked ~~down the aisle towards~~ the dais, and our legs did not tremble, and we looked up at the Council. There were five members of the Council, three of the male gender and two of the female. Their hair was white and their faces were cracked as the clay of a dry river bed. They were old. They seemed older than ~~humans could be, they seemed old as~~ the marble of the Temple of the World Council. They sat before us and they did not move. And we saw no breath to stir the folds of their white togas. But we knew that they were alive, for a finger ~~on the right~~ hand of the oldest rose and fell down again. This was the only thing which moved, for the lips of the oldest did not move as they said: "Street Sweeper."

We felt the ~~tendons~~ of our neck ~~pull~~ as

20

our head rose higher to look upon the faces of the Council, and we were happy. We knew we had been guilty, but now we had a way to atone for it. We would accept our Life Mandate with our whole heart and we would work for our brothers, gladly and willingly, and we would erase our sin against them, which they did not know, but we knew. And we were happy, and proud of ourselves and of our victory over ourselves. So We raised our right arm and we spoke, and our voice was the clearest and the steadiest voice in the hall that day, and we said:

"The will of our brothers be done."

And we looked straight into the eyes of the Council, but their eyes were as cold blue glass buttons.

So we went into the Home of the Street Sweepers. It is a grey house on a narrow street. There is a sun-dial in its courtyard, and by this the Council of the Home can tell the hours of the day and when to ring

the bell. When the bell rings, we all arise from our beds. The sky is green and cold ~~and hard as metal, and a band of gold gleams over the City,~~ in our windows to the east. The shadow on the sun-dial marks off a half-hour while we dress and eat our breakfast in the dining hall, ~~which has three~~ long tables with ~~one hundred~~ clay plates and ~~one hundred~~ clay cups on each table. Then we go to work in the ~~City~~ streets, with our brooms and our rakes. ~~And~~ In five hours, when the sun is high, we return to the Home and we eat our midday meal, for which one half-hour is allowed. Then we go to work again. In five hours, the shadows are blue on the pavements, and the sky is blue with a deep brightness which is not bright. ~~Then~~ We come back to have our dinner, which lasts one hour. Then the bell rings and we walk in a straight column, ~~with the Council of the H[illegible], to the City Park where we stand in rows, and stretch our~~

~~arms and bend our bodies, while the Council beats a drum. This we do in order that our bodies may be healthy and fit and good for work. The sky is [illegible] and soft, spreading [illegible] soggy purple, and the trees are black against the band of bronze in the west. In an hour we return to the Home. Then the bell rings and we walk in a straight column~~ to one of the City Halls, for the Social Meeting. Other columns of men arrive from the Homes of the different Trades. The candles are lit, and the Councils of the different Homes stand in a ~~tall~~ pulpit, and they speak to us of our duties and of our brother men. Then visiting Leaders mount the pulpit and they read to us the speeches which were made in the City Council that day, for the City Council represents all men and all men must know. Then we sing hymns, the Hymn of Brotherhood, and the Hymn of Equality, and the Hymn of the Collective Spirit. ~~Then two hours pass. Then~~ we walk in a straight

The sky is a soggy purple when we return to the Home. Then the bell rings and column to the City Theatre for three hours of Social Recreation. There a play is shown upon the stage, with two great choruses from the Home of the Actors, which speak and answer all together, in two great voices. The plays are about toil and how good it is. Then we walk back to the Home in a straight column. The sky is like a black sieve pierced by silver drops ~~which~~ tremble, ready to burst through. The moths beat against the street lanterns. We go to our beds and we sleep, till the bell rings again. The sleeping halls are white and clean and bare of all things save one hundred beds.

Thus have we lived each day of four years, until two springs ago when our crime happened. Thus must all men live until they are forty. At forty, ~~their bodies are shrunken as dry mushrooms and there are pains in their bones~~. At forty, they are sent to the Home of the Useless, where the Old Ones live. The Old Ones do not work, for the State takes

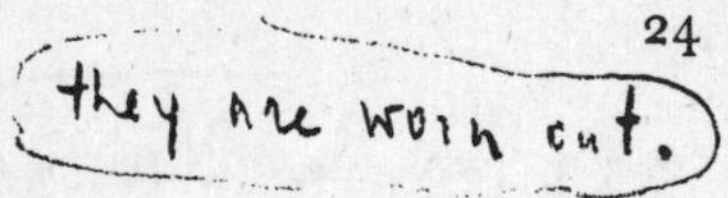

care of them. They sit in the sun in summer and they sit ~~at~~ the fire in winter. They do not speak often, for they are weary, ~~and their eyes water.~~ The Old Ones know that they are soon to die. When a miracle happens and some live to be forty-five, they are the Ancient Ones, and children stare at them when passing by the Home of the Useless. Such is to be our life, as that of all our brothers and of the brothers who came before us.

Such would have been our life, had we not ~~made the discovery and~~ committed our ~~great~~ crime which changed all things for us. And it was our curse which drove us to ~~it.~~ We had been a good Street Sweeper and like all our brother Street Sweepers, save for our cursed wish to know. We looked too long at the stars at night, and at the trees and ~~at~~ the earth ~~under our feet.~~ And when we cleaned the yard of the Home of the Scholars, we gathered the glass vials, ~~and~~

the ~~iron~~ pieces ~~and~~ the dried bones ~~in the refuse~~ they had discarded. We wished to keep these things and to study them, but we had no place ~~in which~~ to hide them. So we carried them to the City Cesspool. And then we made the discovery.

It was on a day of the spring before last. We Street Sweepers work in brigades of three, and we were with Union 5-3992, they of the half-brain, and with International 4-8818. Now Union 5-3992 are a sickly lad and sometimes they are stricken with convulsions, when their mouth froths and their eyes turn white. But International 4-8818 are different. They are a tall, strong youth and their eyes are like fireflies, for ~~they twinkle and~~ there is laughter in ~~them~~. We cannot look upon International 4-8818 and not smile in answer. For this they were not liked in the Home of the Students, as it is not proper to smile without reason. And also they were not liked because they took pieces of coal and they drew pictures upon the walls and upon the floors, and they were pictures which made men laugh. But it is only our brothers in the Home of the Artists who are permitted to draw pictures, so International 4-8818 were sent to the Home of the Street Sweepers, like ourselves. International 4-8818 and we are friends. This is an evil thing to say, for it is a transgression, the great Transgression of Preference, to love any among men better than the others, as we must love all men and all men are our friends. So International 4-8818 and we have never spoken of it. But we know. We know, when we look into each other's eyes. And when we look thus without words, we both know other things also, strange things for which there are no words, and these things frighten us.

So on that day of the spring before last, Union 5-3992 were stricken with convulsions on the edge of the City, near the City

Theatre. We left them to lie in the shade of the Theatre tent and we went with International 4-8818 to finish our work. We came together to the great ravine ~~which is~~ behind the Theatre. It is empty ~~of all things~~ save trees and weeds. ~~It stretches to the hills~~ Beyond~~, and then~~ there is a plain, and beyond the plain there lies the Uncharted Forest, about which men must not think. We were gathering the papers and the rags which the wind had blown from the Theatre ~~And then~~ we saw an iron bar ~~sticking from the earth~~ among the weeds. It was old and rusted by many rains. We pulled with all our strength, but we could not move it. So we called International 4-8818, and together we scraped the earth around the bar. Of a sudden the earth fell in before us, and we saw an old iron grill over a black hole. ~~Beyond the hole there seemed to be darkness without bottom.~~ International 4-8818 ~~trembled and~~ stepped back. But we pulled at the

grill and it gave way. And then we saw iron rings as steps leading into t~~he heart of the earth~~ a darkness without bottom.

"We shall go down," we said to International 4-8818.

"It is forbidden," they answered.

We said: "The Council does not know of this hole, so it cannot be forbidden."

And they answered: "Since the Council does not know of this hole, there can be no law permitting to enter it. And everything which is not permitted by law is forbidden."

But we said: "We shall go, none the less."

They were frightened, ~~so they fell on their knees and looked down, watching~~ us go.

We hung on the iron rings with our hands and our feet. We could see nothing below us, ~~save a night blacker than night~~. And above us the hole open upon the sky grew smaller and smaller, till it came to be the size of a button. ~~But still~~ we went down, ~~and we would have gone on had the shaft been~~

~~without bottom.~~ Then our foot touched the ~~earth, and it was soft and sodden.~~ We rubbed our ~~eyelids~~, for we could not see. Then our eyes became used to the darkness, but we could not believe what we saw. No men known to us could have built this place, nor the men known to our brothers who lived before us, and yet it was built by men. It was a great tunnel, ~~but it had no beginning and no end.~~ Its walls were hard and smooth to the touch; it felt like stone, but it was not stone. ~~And~~ On the ground ~~under our feet~~ there were ~~two pairs of~~ long thin tracks of iron, but it was not iron; it felt smooth and cold as glass. We ~~fell on our knees~~, and we crawled forward, ~~and~~ our hand ~~followed~~ the iron line to see where it would lead. But there was ~~night~~ unbroken ahead. Only the ~~four~~ iron ~~bands~~ glowed through it, ~~as thin streams of water,~~ straight and white, ~~hanging in space,~~ calling us to follow. But we could not follow, for we were losing the puddle of light behind us, so we turned and we crawled back, our hand on the iron line. And our heart beat in our fingertips, ~~in a madness~~ without reason. And then we knew.

We knew suddenly that this place ~~had~~ ~~been~~ left from the Unmentionable Times. So it was true, and those Times had been, and all the wonders of those Times. Hundreds upon hundreds of years ago men knew ~~strange~~ secrets which we have lost. And we thought: "This is a foul place. They are damned who touch the things of the Unmentionable Times." But our hand which followed the track, as we crawled, clung to the iron as if it would not leave it, as if the skin of our hand were thirsty and begging of the metal some secret fluid beating in its coldness. ~~And our hand did this without our will.~~

We ~~came back~~ to ~~the face of~~ the earth. International 4-8818 looked upon us and

~~they~~ stepped back ~~and their lips trembled in terror~~.

"Equality 7-2521," they said, "your face is white ~~and your eyes are not like the eyes of men~~."

But we could not speak and we stood looking upon them.

They backed away, as if they dared not touch us. ~~And~~ Then they smiled, but it was not a gay smile; it was lost and pleading. But still we could not speak. Then they said:

"We shall report our find to the City Council and both of us will be rewarded."

And then we spoke. ~~And~~ Our voice was hard and there was no mercy in our voice. ~~And~~ We said:

"We shall not report our find to the City Council. We shall not report it to any ~~among~~ men."

~~International 4-8818~~ raised their hands to their ears, for never had they heard such words as these.

~~But we looked upon them, without kindness and without shame.~~

"International 4-8818," we asked, "will you report us to the Council and see us lashed to death before your eyes?"

~~Then~~ they stood straight of a sudden and they answered:

"Rather would we die."

"Then," we said, "keep ~~your mouth closed forever about this~~. This place is ours. This place belongs to us, Equality 7-2521, and to no other men on earth. And if ever we surrender it, we shall surrender our life with it also."

~~And~~ then we saw that the eyes of International 4-8818 were ~~glistening and~~ full to the lids with tears they dared not drop. ~~And~~ they ~~said~~, and their voice ~~was only a whisper which~~ trembled, so that their words lost all shape:

"The will of the Council is above all things, for it is the will of our brothers, which is holy. But if you wish it so, we shall obey you. Rather shall we be evil with you than good with all our brothers. May the Council have mercy upon both our hearts!"

Then we walked away together and back to the Home of the Street Sweepers. And we walked in silence.

Thus did it come to pass that each night, when the stars are high and the Street Sweepers sit in the City Theatre, we, Equality 7-2521, steal out and run through the darkness to our place. It is easy to leave the Theatre; ~~we are assigned to a seat on the edge of the last row, next to International 4-8818;~~ when the candles are blown ~~out~~ and the Actors come unto the stage, no eyes can see us as we crawl under our seat and under the cloth of the ~~big Theatre~~ tent. Later, it ~~will be~~ easy to steal through the shadows and ~~to~~ fall in line next to International 4-8818, as the column leaves the Theatre. ~~Now~~ It is dark in the streets and there are no men about, for no men may walk through the City when they have no mission to walk there. ~~We~~ run ~~down~~ the ravine and ~~the earth flies under our feet. We~~ remove the stones which we have piled upon the iron grill to hide it from ~~all eyes.~~ ~~And then~~ we are under the earth, alone.

We have stolen candles from the ~~larder of~~ the Home, ~~and~~ we have stolen flints, and knives, and paper, ~~which we carried all day in our tunic till~~ we brought them to this place. We have stolen glass vials, and powders, and acids, ~~and iron retorts~~ from the Home of the Scholars, ~~when we cleaned its yard and reached in through its open windows. We have done these things in order that we may study~~. Now we sit in the tunnel for three ~~evil, blessed~~ hours each night and we ~~learn about the mysteries of the earth~~. We melt strange metals and we mix acids and we cut open the bodies of the animals ~~and the birds~~ which we find in the

35

Each night, for three hours,

City Cesspool. We have built ~~a great~~ oven of the ~~stray~~ bricks we gathered in the streets. We burn the ~~sticks~~ we find in the ravine. The fire flickers in the oven and blue shadows dance upon the walls and there is no sound of men ~~or beasts~~ to disturb us.

We have stolen manuscripts. This is a great offence. Manuscripts are precious, for our brothers in the Home of the Clerks spend one year to copy one single script in their clear, ~~exact~~ handwritings. Manuscripts are rare and they are kept in the Home of the Scholars. So we sit ~~by the oven~~ and we read the stolen scripts. Two years have passed since we found this place. And in these two years we have learned more than we had learned in the ten years of the Home of the Students.

We have learned things which are not in the scripts. We have ~~found~~ secrets of which the Scholars have no knowledge. We have come to see ~~that~~ great is ~~the unknown and~~

be

the unexplored, and many lifetimes will not bring us to the end of our quest. But we wish no end to our quest. We wish ~~nothing~~, save to ~~sit~~ alone ~~by our own~~ and to learn ~~from the things of the earth~~, and to feel as if with each day our sight were growing sharper than the hawk's and clearer than rock crystal.

Strange are the ways of evil. We are false in the faces of our brothers. We are defying the will of our Councils. We alone, of the thousands ~~and thousands~~ who walk this earth, we alone in this hour are doing a work ~~which no men have bid us to do. The depth of~~ our crime is not for the human mind to probe. The nature of our punishment, if it be discovered, is not for the human heart to ponder. Never, not in the memory of the Ancient Ones' Ancients, never have men done ~~the thing~~ which we are doing. that

And yet there is no shame in us and no regret. We say to ourselves that we are a

37

which has no purpose save that we want to do it. The evil of wretch and a traitor. But we feel no burden upon our spirit and no fear in our heart. And it seems to us that our spirit is clear as a lake troubled by no eyes save those of the sun. And in our heart—strange are the ways of evil!—in our heart there is the first peace we have known in twenty years.

~~[illegible]~~

II

LIBERTY 5-3000 . . . Liberty five-three thousand . . . Liberty 5-3000 . . .

We ~~rejoice in writing~~ wish to write this name. We ~~re-joice in speaking~~ wish to speak it, but we dare not speak it above a whisper. For men are forbidden to take notice of women, and women are forbidden to take notice of men. But we think of one among women, they whose name is Liberty 5-3000, and we think of no others.

The women who have been assigned to work the soil live in the Homes of the Peasants beyond the City. Where the City ends there is a great road winding off to the north, and we Street Sweepers must keep this road clean to the first milepost. There is a hedge, ~~green and long~~ along the road,

39

and beyond the hedge ~~lie~~ the fields, ~~[illegible]~~ ~~[illegible]~~. The fields are black and ploughed, and they lie like a great fan before us, with their furrows gathered in some hand ~~[illegible]~~ beyond the ~~horizon, and~~ spreading forth from that hand, ~~and~~ opening wide apart as they come toward us, black pleats ~~sparkling~~ with thin, green spangles. Women work in the fields, ~~and they walk and bend, sixty paces apart from one another,~~ and their white tunics in the wind are like the wings of sea-gulls beating over the black ~~field~~ soil.

And there it was that we saw Liberty 5-3000 walking along the furrows. Their body was straight ~~and strong~~ and thin as a blade of iron. Their eyes were dark and hard and glowing, with no fear in them ~~and~~ no kindness and no ~~shame~~. Their hair ~~was like no hair of men nor women; their hair~~ was golden as the sun; their hair flew in the wind, ~~trembling and sparkling~~ and wild, ~~free and defiant in its freedom.~~ They threw seeds

40

as if it defied men to restrain it.

from their hand as if they deigned to fling a scornful gift, and the earth was as a beggar under their feet.

~~Thus did Liberty 5-3000 walk toward us in the field that day, as a thin flame in the wind, as a swaying white mist, as a scourge, as a miracle. And~~ we stood still, ~~and we knew of nothing save our eyes which were seeing this. And~~ for the first time did we know fear, ~~in our heart~~, and then pain. And we stood still that we may not spill this pain more precious than pleasure.

Then ~~they came to the end of the furrow, and they turned and walked back~~. We heard a voice from the others call their name: "Liberty 5-3000," and they turned and ~~then~~ walked ~~[illegible]~~. Thus we learned their name, and we stood watching them go, till their white tunic was lost in the blue mist.

And the following day, as we came to the northern road, we kept our eyes upon Liberty ~~5-3000 in the field~~. And each day thereafter

41

we knew the illness of ~~waiting, and our body ached with the~~ waiting for our hour on the northern road. And there we looked upon Liberty 5-3000 each day. We know not whether they looked upon us also, but we think they did.

Then one day they came close to the hedge, and they turned ~~suddenly and looked straight upon us~~. They turned in a whirl and the movement of their body stopped, as if slashed off, as suddenly as it had started. They stood still as a stone, ~~their body thrown back, their arms flung out and frozen.~~ And ~~they~~ looked straight upon us, straight into our eyes. There was no smile on their face, ~~and no cheers,~~ and no welcome. But their face was taut, and their eyes were dark ~~and wide~~. Then they turned as swiftly, and they walked away, ~~and they walked faster than we had ever seen them walk~~.

But the following day, ~~they looked upon us~~ when we came to the road, ~~and~~ they smiled. They smiled to us and for us. ~~Their lips were soft and glistening in the sun~~. And we smiled in answer. ~~They turned away slowly, and~~ their head fell back, and their arms fell ~~limply~~, as if their arms and their thin white neck were stricken suddenly with a great lassitude. They were not looking upon us, but upon the sky. ~~And~~ then they glanced at us over their shoulder, ~~and that glance was soft and heavy~~, and we felt as if a hand had touched our body, slipping softly from our lips to our feet. ~~Then they walked away, [illegible]~~ morning thereafter, ~~Liberty 5-3000 and~~ we greeted each other with our eyes. We dared not speak. It is a ~~great~~ transgression to speak to men of other Trades, save in groups at the Social Meetings. But once, standing at the hedge, we ~~dared to raise~~ our hand to our forehead and then move it slowly, palm down, toward Liberty 5-3000. Had the others seen it, they could have guessed nothing, for it looked only as

43

if we were shading our eyes from the sun. But Liberty 5-3000 saw it and understood. ~~And~~ they raised their hand to their forehead and moved it as we had. Thus, each day, ~~do~~ we greet Liberty 5-3000, and they answer, and no men can suspect.

~~Evil begets evil. So we~~ wonder ~~not~~ at this new sin of ours. It is our second Transgression of Preference, for we think ~~not~~ of all our brothers, as we must, but only of one, and their name is Liberty 5-3000. We know ~~not~~ why we think of them. We know ~~not~~ ~~why~~, when we think of them, we feel of a sudden that the earth is good and that it is not a burden to live. ~~And the curse in us cries in a voice of thunder that we would rather see all our brothers, yes, all the thousands and thousands of them, die in agonies unspeakable than see one golden hair hurt on the head of Liberty 5-3000. And these words, which should burn the paper we write them on by the fire~~

~~of their evil, these words frighten us not.~~

We think ~~not~~ of them as Liberty 5-3000 any longer. We have given them a name in our thoughts. We call them the Golden One. But it is ~~the~~ sin ~~of sins~~ to give men names which distinguish them from other men. Yet we call them the Golden One, for they are not like the others. The Golden One are not like the others. ~~*The Golden One are not like the others!* Thus do we wish to scream in the pride of our sin.~~

And we take no heed of the law which says that men ~~are to receive one hundred lashes, if they are found to be taking notice of any one among women, and if they survive the lashes, they are sent for ten years to the Palace of Corrective Detention. Men~~ may not think of women, save at the Time of Mating. This is the time each spring when all the men older than twenty and all the women older than eighteen are sent for one night to the City Palaces of Mating. And each of the

45

men have one of the women assigned to them by the Council of Eugenics. Children are born each winter, but women never see their children and children never know their parents. Twice have we been sent to the Palace of Mating, but it is ~~a thing~~ ugly and shameful of which we do not like to think. To-day we spoke to the Golden One.

The other women were far off in the field, when we stopped at the hedge by the side of the road. The Golden One were kneeling alone at the moat which runs through the field. And the drops falling from ~~the~~ hands ~~of the Golden One~~ as they raised water to their lips, were like sparks of fire in the sun. ~~We looked upon~~ the Golden One ~~and they felt our glance. They raised their head to us~~, and they did not move, kneeling there, looking upon us, and circles of light played upon their white tunic, from the sun on the water of the moat, and one sparkling drop fell from a finger of their hand held as frozen in the air.

Then the Golden One rose and walked ~~slowly~~ to the hedge, as if they had heard a command in our eyes. The two other Street Sweepers of our brigade were a hundred paces away down the road. And we thought that International 4-8818 would not betray us, and Union 5-3992 would not understand. So we looked straight upon the Golden One, and we saw the shadows of their lashes ~~on~~ their white cheeks and the ~~little~~ spark of sun on their lips. And ~~then~~ we ~~spoke. We~~ said:

"You are beautiful, Liberty 5-3000."

~~Never have men spoken thus unto women. But the Golden One were not frightened.~~ Their face did not move and they did not avert their eyes. Only their eyes grew wider ~~[illegible]~~ and there was triumph in their eyes, and it was not triumph over us, but over things we could not guess.

Then they asked:

"What is your name?"

"Equality 7-2521," we answered.

~~They said, and we saw a blue thread trembling under the white skin of their throat.~~

"You are not one of our brothers, Equality 7-2521, for we do not wish you to be."

We cannot say what they meant, for there are no words for their meaning, but we know it without words and we knew it then.

"No," we answered, "nor are you one of our sisters."

"If you see us among scores of women," ~~they asked,~~ will you look upon us?"

"We shall look upon you, Liberty 5-3000," ~~we answered,~~ if we ~~are to be lashed to death for it.~~ see you among all the women of the earth."

Then they asked:

"Are Street Sweepers sent to different ~~quarters~~ parts of the City or do they always work in the same places?"

"They always work in the same places," we answered, "and no one will take this road away from us. ~~Your hair, Liberty 5-3000," we asked, "does it glow in the night and light the hall where you sleep?"~~

~~"No," they answered, "but your eyes are glowing.~~ Your eyes are not like the eyes of any among men."

And suddenly, without cause ~~or connection~~ for the thought which came to us, we felt cold, cold to our stomach.

"How old are you?" we asked.

They understood our thought, for they lowered their eyes for the first time, ~~and the pale cheeks of them who knew no fear blushed suddenly.~~

"Seventeen," they whispered.

And we sighed, as if a burden had been taken from us, for we had been thinking without reason of the Palace of Mating. And we thought ~~suddenly~~ that we would not let the Golden One be sent to the Palace ~~of Mating~~. How to prevent it, how to bar the will of the Councils, we knew not, but we knew suddenly that we would. Only we know ~~not~~ why such thought came to us, for these ugly matters bear no relation to us and the Golden One. What relation can they bear?

Still, without reason, as we stood there by the ~~hedge,~~ we felt our lips drawn tight ~~and hard~~ with ~~sudden~~ hatred, a hatred for all our brother men. And the Golden One ~~looked upon us~~ and smiled slowly, and there was in their smile the first sadness we had seen in them. We think that in the wisdom of women the Golden One had understood more than we can understand.

Then three of the sisters in the field appeared, coming toward the road, so the Golden One ~~turned and~~ walked away from us. ~~We saw the Golden One pick up~~ the bag of seeds, and they threw the seeds into the furrows of earth as they walked away. But the seeds flew wildly, for the hand of the Golden One was trembling.

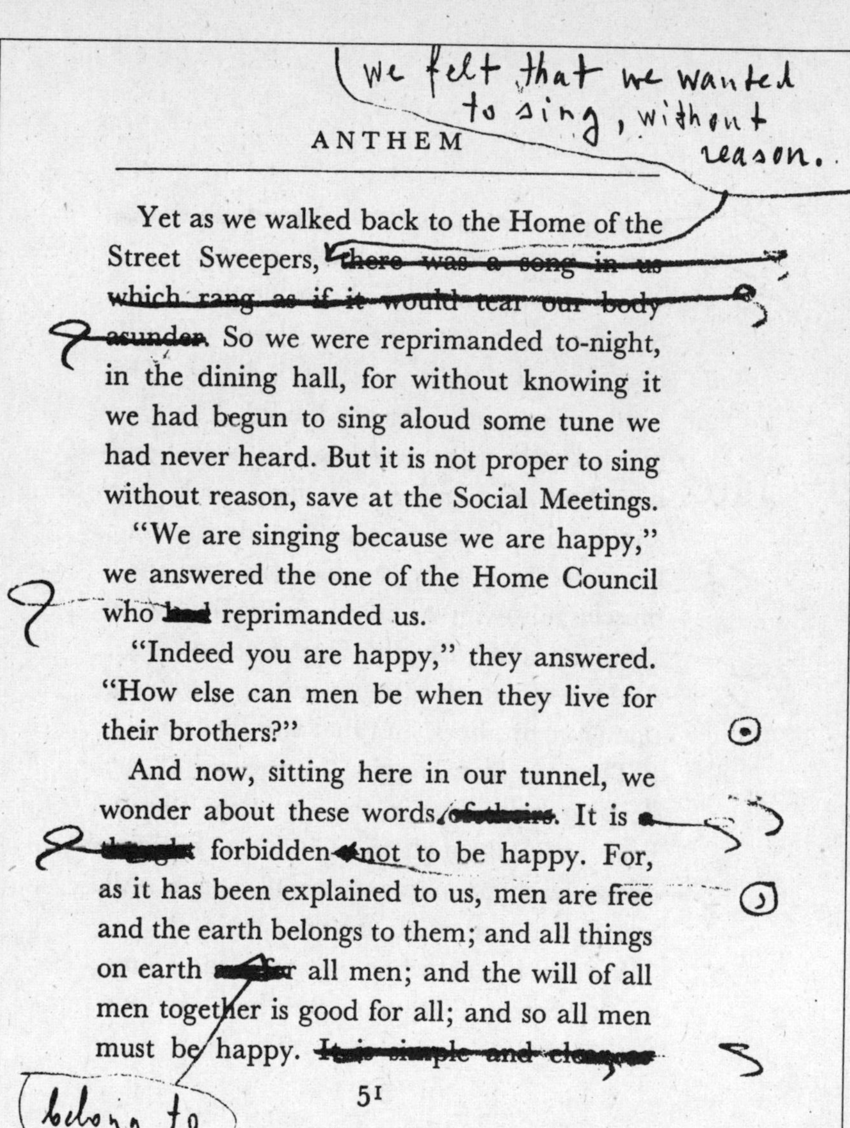

we felt that we wanted to sing, without reason.

ANTHEM

Yet as we walked back to the Home of the Street Sweepers, ~~there was a song in us which rang as if it would tear our body asunder~~. So we were reprimanded to-night, in the dining hall, for without knowing it we had begun to sing aloud some tune we had never heard. But it is not proper to sing without reason, save at the Social Meetings.

"We are singing because we are happy," we answered the one of the Home Council who ~~had~~ reprimanded us.

"Indeed you are happy," they answered. "How else can men be when they live for their brothers?"

And now, sitting here in our tunnel, we wonder about these words ~~of theirs~~. It is ~~a thought~~ forbidden not to be happy. For, as it has been explained to us, men are free and the earth belongs to them; and all things on earth ~~are~~ for all men; and the will of all men together is good for all; and so all men must be happy. ~~It is simple and clear~~

51

belong to

~~water, and men have never doubted it,~~
~~for no men are born save happy men.~~

Yet as we stand at night in the great hall, removing our garments for sleep, we look upon our brothers and we wonder. The heads of our brothers are bowed. The eyes of our brothers are ~~not clean, but veiled and~~ dull, ~~[illegible]~~ and never do they look one another in the eyes. The shoulders of our brothers are hunched ~~[illegible]~~, and their muscles are drawn, as if their bodies were shrinking and wished to shrink out of sight. ~~And a~~ word steals into our mind, as we look upon our brothers, and that word is fear.

There is fear hanging in the air of the sleeping halls, and in the air of the streets. Fear walks through the City, fear ~~without~~ ~~[illegible]~~ without name, without shape. All men feel it and none dare to speak.

We feel it also, when we are in the Home of the Street Sweepers. But here, in our tunnel, we feel it no longer. The air is pure

52

under the earth. There is no odour of men here, and we feel clean as clean as if we had stepped out of a bath.

Our body is betraying us, for the Council of the Home looks with suspicion upon us. It is not good to feel too much joy in our body nor to be glad that our body lives. For we matter not and it must not matter to us whether we live or die, which is to be as our brothers will it. But we, Equality 7-2521, rejoice to be living. If it be sin, then we wish no virtue.

Yet our brothers are not like us. The air is heavy in the sleeping halls and all is not well with our brothers. There are Fraternity 2-5503, a quiet lad with wise, kind eyes, who cry suddenly, without reason, in the midst of day or night, and their body shakes with sobs they cannot explain. There are Solidarity 9-6347, who are a bright youth, glad and without fear in the day; but they scream in their sleep, and they scream:

"Help us! Help us! Help us!" into the night, in a voice which chills ~~the marrow of~~ our bones, but the Doctors cannot cure Solidarity 9-6347.

And as we all undress at night, in the dim ~~glow~~ light of the candles, our brothers are silent, for they dare not speak the thoughts of their minds. For all must agree with all, and they cannot know if their thoughts are the thoughts of all, and so they fear to speak. And they are glad when the candles are blown for the night. But we, Equality 7-2521, look through the window upon the sky, and there is peace in the sky, and cleanliness, and dignity. And beyond the City there lies the plain, and beyond the plain, black upon the black sky, there lies the Uncharted Forest.

We do not wish to look upon the Uncharted Forest. We do not wish to think of it. But ever do our eyes return to that black ~~line~~ patch upon the sky. Men never enter the Uncharted Forest, for there is no power to explore it and no path to lead among its ancient trees which stand~~, sombre and evil,~~ as guards of secrets ~~unspeakable~~. It is whispered that once or twice in a hundred years, one among the men of the City escape alone and run to the Uncharted Forest, without call or reason. These men do not return. They perish from hunger and from the claws of the wild beasts which roam the Forest. But our Councils say that this is only a legend. We have heard that there are many Uncharted Forests over the land, among the Cities. And it is whispered that they have grown over the ruins of many cities of the Unmentionable Times. The trees have swallowed the ruins, and the bones under the ruins, and all the things which perished.

And as we look upon the Uncharted Forest far in the night, we think of the secrets of the Unmentionable Times. And we wonder how it came to pass that these secrets were lost to the world. We have heard the legends of the great fighting, in which many men fought on one side and only a few on the other. These few were the Evil Ones and they were conquered. ~~And~~ then great fires raged over the land. And in these fires the Evil Ones and all the things made by the Evil Ones were burned. And the fire ~~[illegible]~~ which is called the Dawn of the Great Re-birth, was the ~~[illegible]~~ Fire where all the scripts of the Evil Ones were burned, and with them all the words of the Evil Ones. ~~[illegible]~~ Great mountains of flame stood in the squares of the Cities for three months ~~and a day.~~ Then came the Great Re-birth.

The words of the Evil Ones . . . The words of the Unmentionable Times . . . What are the words which we have lost?

~~Great Mercy of all human mercies, have pity upon us!~~ We had no wish to write such question, and we knew not what we were doing till we had written it. We shall not ask

56

¶ May the Council have mercy upon us!

this question and we shall not think it. We shall not call death upon our head.

And yet . . . And yet . . .

There is some word, one single word which is not in the language of men, but which had been. And this is the Unspeakable Word, which no men may speak ~~and no men may~~ nor hear. But sometimes, and it is rare, sometimes, somewhere, one among men find that Word. They find it upon scraps of old manuscripts or cut into the fragments of ancient stones. But when they speak it they are put to death. There is no crime punished by death in this world, save this one crime of speaking the Unspeakable Word.

We have seen one of such men burned alive in the square of the City. And it was a sight which has stayed with us through the years, and it haunts us, and follows us, and it gives us no rest. We were a child then, ten years old. And we stood in the great square with all the children and all the men of the

City, sent to behold the burning. ~~And~~ They brought the Transgressor out into the square and they led them to the ~~great~~ pyre. They had torn out the tongue of the Transgressor, so that they could speak no longer. The Transgressor were young and tall. They had hair of gold and eyes blue as morning. They walked to the pyre, and their step did not falter, ~~and there was a pride in them and a calm which [illegible] understanding.~~ And of all the faces on that square, of all the faces which shrieked and screamed and spat curses upon them, theirs was the calmest and the happiest face.

As the chains were wound over their body at the stake, and a flame set to ~~[illegible]~~ the pyre, the Transgressor looked upon the City. There was a thin thread of blood running from the corner of their mouth, but their lips ~~[illegible]~~ were smiling. And a monstrous thought came to us then, which has never left us. We had heard of Saints. There are the Saints of

58

Labour, and the Saints of the Councils, and the Saints of the Great Re-birth. But we had never seen a Saint nor what the likeness of a Saint should be. And we thought then, standing in the square, that the likeness of a Saint was the face we saw before us in the flames, the face of the Transgressor of the Unspeakable Word.

As the flames rose, a thing happened which no eyes saw but ours, else we would not be living to-day. Perhaps it had only seemed to us. But it seemed to us that the eyes of the Transgressor had chosen us from the crowd and were looking straight upon us. There was no pain in their eyes and no knowledge of the agony of their body. There was only joy in them, a joy holier than it is fit for human joy to be. And it seemed as if these eyes were trying to tell us something through the flames, to send into our eyes some word without sound. And it seemed as if these eyes were begging us to gather that word and not to let it go from us and from the earth. But the flames rose and we could not guess the word . . .

What—even if we have to burn for it like the Saint of the pyre—what is the Unspeakable Word?

III

TO-NIGHT, we shall write it down upon this paper, and face it and acknowledge it, even though we are afraid. We shall write down the thought which has tortured us for two years. It has been coming to us, even though we tried not to know it and not to listen. And while we said to ourselves that we held no such thought, it formed itself into words, and the words rang in our ears as a bell of alarm within our mind.

So now we shall say it openly to ourselves, and it is this: We, Equality 7-2521, have discovered a new power of nature. And we have discovered it alone, and we are alone to know it.

61

are not known by all

lashed

It is said. Now let us be ~~put to death~~ for it, if we must. The Council of Scholars has said that we all know the things which exist and therefore the things which ~~we do not know~~ do not exist. But we think that the Council of Scholars is blind. The secrets of this earth are ~~without end, and they are~~ not for all men to see, but only for such as will seek them. We know, for we have found a secret unknown to all our brothers.

We know not what this power is nor whence it comes. But we know its nature, ~~and~~ we have watched it and worked with it. We saw it first two years ago. One night, ~~not long after we had begun to come here for study,~~ we were cutting open the body of a dead frog when we saw its leg jerking. It was dead, yet it moved. Some power unknown to men was making it move. ~~We stood awed and stricken before it. And for many days we thought of it. And~~ then, after many tests, we found the answer. The frog had been

We could not understand it.

hanging on a wire of copper; and it had been the metal of our knife which had sent a strange power to the copper through the brine ~~in~~ the frog's body. We put a piece of copper and piece of zinc into a jar of brine, ~~and~~ we touched a wire to them, and ~~we felt a shock which was not like a blow and not like fire, but like no feeling for which there is a name. And we touched it again, and we bore the pain of it gladly, for~~ there, under our fingers, was a miracle which had never occurred ~~upon~~ earth, a new miracle and a new power.

~~And~~ This discovery haunted us. ~~In~~ preference to all our studies ~~we came back to it again and again~~. We worked with it, we tested it in more ways than we can describe, and each step was as another miracle unveiling before us. ~~And~~ We came to know that we had found the greatest power ~~upon this~~ earth. For it defies all laws known to men. ~~We found that~~ It makes the needle move and turn on the compass which we stole from the Home of the Scholars; but we had been taught, when still a child, that the loadstone points to the north and that this is a law ~~of the earth~~ which nothing can change; yet our new power defies ~~this law of the earth, and~~ all ~~the~~ laws ~~of heaven~~. We found that it causes lightning, and never have men known what causes lightning. In thunderstorms, we raised a tall rod of iron by the side of our hole, and we watched it from below. We have seen the lightning strike it again and again. And now we know that metal draws the power of the sky, and that metal can be made to give it forth.

We have built strange ~~engines and done many things inconceivable~~ with this discovery of ours. We used for it the copper wires which we found here under the ground. We have walked the length of our tunnel, with a candle ~~in our hand~~ lighting the way. ~~But~~ We could go no farther than half a mile, for ~~the~~ earth and ~~the~~ rocks had fallen at both ends~~, and no might of men could break a way through~~. But we gathered all the things ~~which~~ we found and we brought them to our work place. ~~And~~ We found strange boxes with bars of metal inside, with many cords and strands and coils of metal. We found wires~~, more wires than we had ever seen~~ before~~. The wires~~ led to strange little ~~balls of glass~~ on the wall~~. The balls were sealed with metal, and inside them there were~~ threads of ~~iron~~ thinner than a spider's web.

These things help us in our work. We understand them ~~not~~, but we think that the men of the Unmentionable Times had known our power of the sky, and ~~that~~ these things ~~have~~ some ~~connection with~~ it. We know ~~it not~~, but we shall learn. We cannot stop now, even though ~~the thought~~ frightens us that we are alone in our knowledge. No single one can possess greater wisdom than the many Scholars who are elected by all men for their wisdom. Yet we can. We do. We have fought against saying it, too long, and now it is said. We care not. We forget all men, all questions, all things save our metals, our wires and our words. So much is still to be learned! So long a road lies before us, and what care we if we must travel it alone!

Now we look upon these words and we cannot believe that our hand has written them. It cannot be, we cannot be as evil as this. But we are. If only, we pray, if only we could suffer as we say this. Could we but suffer remorse, we would know that there is a spark of good left in us. But we suffer not. Our hand is light. Our hand and the thought which drives our hand to write, laugh at us and know no shame.

~~CHAPTER~~

IV

MANY days passed before we could speak to the Golden One again. But then came the day when the sky turned ~~to~~ white ~~fire~~, as if the sun had burst and spread its flame ~~over the earth~~ *in the air,* and the fields lay still without breath, and the dust of the road was white in the glow. So the women of the field were weary, and they tarried over their work, and they were far from the road when we came. But the Golden One stood alone at the hedge, ~~leaning on the green boughs, calm and still and~~ waiting. We stopped ~~before them~~ and ~~we looked upon the Golden One. And~~ we saw that their eyes, so hard and scornful to the world, were suddenly soft and humble, as if they would obey any word we may speak.

And we said:

"We have given you a name in our thoughts, Liberty 5-3000."

"What is our name?" they asked.

"The Golden One," we answered.

"Nor do we call you Equality 7-2521 when we think of you," they whispered. We asked: "What name have you given us?"

They looked straight into our eyes and they held their head high and they answered:

"The Unconquered."

For a long time we could not speak. Then we said:

"Such thoughts as these are forbidden, Golden One."

"Then we should be forbidden to look upon you also," they answered. "Then you should be forbidden, you and your body and the look of your eyes. For you think such thoughts as these and you wish us to think them."

~~And~~ We looked into their eyes and we could not lie.

"Yes," we whispered, and they smiled, and then we said: "Our dearest one, do not obey us."

They stepped back ~~and looked upon us~~ and their eyes were wide and still.

"Speak these words again," they whispered.

"Which words?" we asked. But they did not answer ~~them~~, and we knew ~~, and their eyes were burning.~~ it.

"Our dearest one," we whispered.

~~Never had we thought of such words and we know not how they came to us, for men do not speak thus unto women.~~

~~The Golden One stood looking upon us, and then they lowered their eyes, and their head~~ bowed slowly, and they stood still before us, their arms ~~limp~~ at their sides, the

69

¶ Never have men said this to women.

¶ The head of the Golden One

palms of their hands turned to us, as if their body were delivered in submission to ~~the will o~~f our eyes. And we could not speak.

Then they raised their head, ~~and smiled softly~~, and they spoke simply and gently, as if they wished us to forget some anxiety of their own.

"The day is hot," they said, "and you have worked for many hours and you must be weary."

"No," we answered.

"It is cooler in the fields," they said, "and there is water to drink. Are you thirsty?"

"Yes," we answered, "but we cannot cross the hedge."

"We shall bring the water to you," they said.

Then they knelt by the moat ~~and~~ they gathered water in their two hands, ~~and~~ they rose and held the water out to our lips.

We know ~~not~~ if we drank that water. We only knew suddenly that their hands were empty, but we were still holding our lips to their hands, and that they knew it, but did not move.

Then we raised our head and stepped back. For we had not known our body and the strange [illegible] of our body, but we knew it then.

And the Golden One stepped back, and held their arms bent before them, and stood looking upon their hands in wonder. Then, [illegible], the Golden One moved away, even though no others were coming, and they moved stepping back, as if they could not turn from us, their arms bent before them, as if they could not lower their hands. And we turned and walked away, without watching them go.

But since that day, whenever there are other women about as we pass on the road and cannot approach them, the Golden One lean their arm over the hedge, and then turn away from us, as if they did not see us.

71

For we did not understand what had made us do this, and we were afraid to understand it.

And we pass by, not looking upon them, as if we took no notice; but, in passing, our hand brushes the hand of the Golden One as it hangs over the hedge.

72

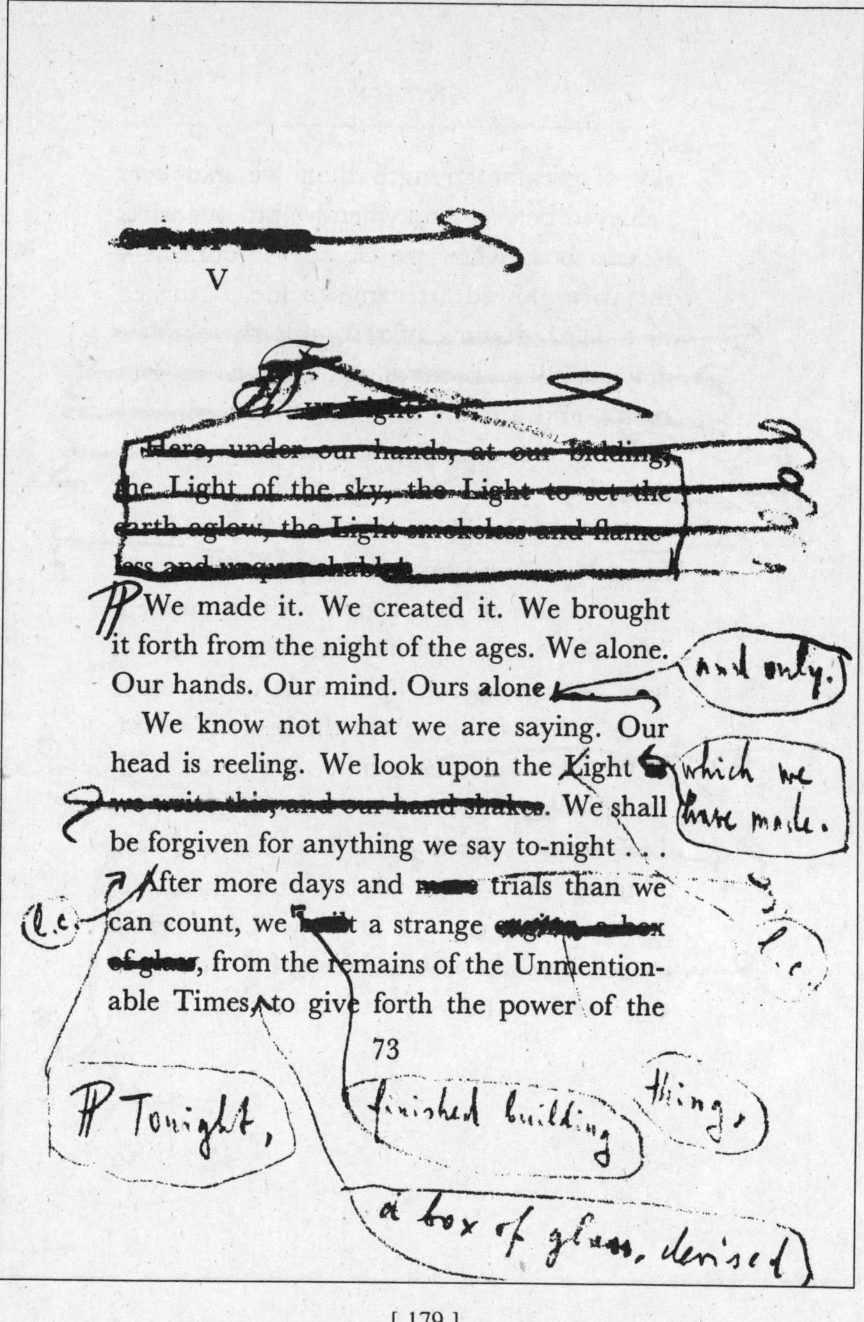

V

~~Here, under our hands, at our bidding, the Light of the sky, the Light to set the earth aglow, the Light smokeless and flameless and unquenchable.~~

We made it. We created it. We brought it forth from the night of the ages. We alone. Our hands. Our mind. Ours alone.

We know not what we are saying. Our head is reeling. We look upon the Light ~~we write this, and our hand shakes~~. We shall be forgiven for anything we say to-night . . .

After more days and ~~more~~ trials than we can count, we ~~built~~ a strange ~~engine, a box of glass~~, from the remains of the Unmentionable Times, to give forth the power of the

73

sky of greater strength than we had ever achieved before. And when we put our wires to this box, when we closed the current— the wire glowed! It came to life, it turned ~~to a faint shadow of red, and the shadow grew, and it became~~ red, ~~red as molten metal~~, and a circle of light lay ~~as a glowing plate~~ before us, ~~upon the stone under the wire.~~

We stood, and we held our head in our hands~~, and our breath stopped.~~ We could not conceive of that which we had created. We had touched no flint, made no fire. Yet here, ~~before us~~ was light, light which came from nowhere, light from the heart of metal.

We blew out ~~our~~ candle. Blackness swallowed ~~all things around~~ us, ~~as a pit which had opened. And~~ there was nothing left, nothing save night and a thin thread of flame in it, as a crack in the wall of a prison ~~into the great day beyond. And~~ we stretched our hands to the wire, and we saw our fingers

~~and our skin, and each line upon our skin~~ in the red glow. ~~There was no sound anywhere.~~ We could not see our body nor feel it, and in that moment nothing existed save our two hands over a wire glowing in a black abyss.

~~And our head reeled as~~ we thought of the meaning of that which lay before us. We can light our tunnel, and the City, and all the Cities of the world with nothing save metal and wires. We can give our brothers a new light, cleaner, brighter than any they have ever known. The power of the sky can be made to do men's bidding. ~~We know so little of it as yet, but one thing we do know and it is this: that~~ there are no limits to ~~the~~ secrets and ~~the~~ might ~~of this power,~~ and ~~that~~ it can be made to grant us ~~things undreamed~~ if we but choose to ask.

~~And~~ then ~~we leapt to our feet, for~~ we knew what we must do. Our discovery is too great to waste our time in sweeping the streets. We must not keep our secret to ourselves, nor buried under the ground. We must bring it into the sight of all men. We need all our time, we need the ~~[illegible]~~ rooms ~~and the engines~~ of the Home of the Scholars, we want the help of our brother Scholars and their wisdom joined to ours. There is so much work ahead for all of us, for all the Scholars of the world~~, and for all the generations of Scholars to come after us~~.

In a month, the World Council of Scholars is to meet in our City. It is a great Council, to which the wisest of all lands are elected, and it meets once a year in the different Cities of the earth. We shall go to this Council and we shall lay before them, as our gift, the glass box with the power of the sky. We shall confess everything to them. They will see, understand and forgive. For our gift is greater than our transgression. They will explain it to the Council of Vocations, and we shall be assigned to the Home of the Scholars. This has never been done before, but neither has a gift such as ours ever been offered to men.

We must wait. We must guard our tunnel as we had never guarded it before. For should any men save the Scholars learn of our secret, they would not grasp it, nor would they believe us. They would see nothing, save our crime of working alone, and they would destroy us and our Light. We care not about our body, but our Light is . . .

Yes, we do care. For the first time do we care about our body. For this wire is as a part of our body, as a vein torn from us, glowing with our blood. Are we proud of this thread of metal, or of our hands which made it, or is there a line to divide these two?

We stretch out our arms and we look upon them. And for the first time do we know how strong our arms are. And a strange thought comes to us: we wonder, for the first time in our life, what we look like. Men

never see their own faces and never ask their brothers about this, for it is evil to have concern for their own faces or bodies. But to-night, for a reason we cannot fathom, we wish it were possible to us to know the likeness of our own person.

This is vain and base, for we are nothing. But are we? Are we? What is this new pride which rises as a fog to strangle the breath in our throat, and as a song, to [illegible] What has befallen us? But what matters it? This Light is above all things. And the being of whom it is born . . . Oh, what matters it? We raise our arms over the flaming wire, we throw our head back, and our spirit is as a hymn within us. We hold the Light, we, Equality 7-2521.

Whatever we are, we hold the Light!

78

VI

WE have not written for thirty days. For thirty days we have not been here, in our tunnel. We had been caught.

It happened on that night when we wrote last. ~~In our joy and in our gladness~~ We forgot, that night, to watch the sand in the glass which tells us when three hours have passed and it is time to return to the City Theatre. When we remembered it, the sand had run out.

We hastened to the Theatre. But the big tent stood grey and silent against the sky. The streets of the City lay before us, dark ~~and wide~~ and empty. If we went back to hide in our tunnel, we would be found and our ~~tunnel~~ light found with us. So we f

79

walked to the Home of the Street Sweepers. And When the Council of the Home questioned us, we looked upon the faces of the Council, but there was no curiosity in those faces, and no anger, and no mercy. So when the oldest of them asked us: "Where have you been?" we thought of our glass box and our Light, and we forgot all else. And we answered:

"We will not tell you."

The oldest did not question us further. They turned to the two youngest, and said, and their voice was bored:

"Take our brother Equality 7-2521 to the Palace of Corrective Detention. Lash them until they tell."

So we were taken to the Stone Room under the Palace of Corrective Detention. This room has no windows and it is empty of all things save an iron post. Two men stood by the post, naked save for leather aprons and leather hoods over their faces. Those who had brought us departed, leaving us to the two Judges who stood in a corner of the room. The Judges were small, thin men, grey and bent. ~~Their little hands shook and their lips were moist~~. They gave the signal to the two strong hooded ones.

They tore our clothes from our body ~~and~~ they threw us down upon our knees and they tied our hands to the iron post.

The first blow of the lash felt as ~~[illegible]~~ if ~~[illegible] cut into our flesh, and the [illegible] from it as a mantle over our body, to the tips of our toes, and [illegible]~~ our spine had been cut in two. The second blow ~~[illegible]~~ and for a ~~[illegible]~~ second we ~~could feel~~ felt nothing, ~~and~~ then the pain struck us in our throat and fire ran in our lungs without air. But we did not cry out.

The lash whistled like a ~~thin~~, singing wind. We tried to count the blows, but we lost count. ~~We felt once as if iron teeth had rip~~

stopped the first.

ped our thigh open, and then our chest, but we knew that the blows were falling upon our back. Only we felt nothing upon our back any longer. And a flaming grill was dancing before our eyes, and we knew nothing save a grill, a grill, a grill of red squares, and then we knew that we were looking upon the squares of the iron grill in the door, and there were also the squares of the stones on the walls, and the squares we felt the lash cutting upon our back, crossing and re-crossing itself in our flesh. And then we felt a thin trickle, heavy and warm, from our waist, running down our legs. But we did not cry out.

Then we saw a huge fist before us, but it was only the small fist of one of the Judges. It knocked our chin up, and we saw the red froth of our mouth upon the withered gray fingers, and the Judges asked:

"Where have you been?"

But we jerked our head away, and hid our

face upon our tied hands, and bit our lips.

~~Then~~ the lash whistled again~~, and we thought we were floating, floating away, and that soft thing writhing upon the stones concerned us not any longer~~. We wondered who was sprinkling burning coal dust upon the floor, for we saw ~~little red beads lighting and dying, and~~ twinkling on the stones around us. ~~We wondered whence that strange sound was coming, the dull sound of a stick beating upon a soft, wet mud.~~

Then we knew nothing, save two voices snarling steadily, ~~without stopping,~~ one after the other, even though we knew they were speaking many minutes apart:

"Where have you been where have you been where have you been where have you been..."

And our lips moved, but the sound trickled back into our throat, and the sound was only:

83

"The Light . . . The Light . . . The Light . . ."

Then we knew nothing.

We opened our eyes, lying upon our stomach on the brick floor of a cell. We looked upon two hands lying far before us on the bricks, and we moved them, and we knew that they were our hands. But we could not move our body. Then we smiled, for we thought of the Light and that we had not betrayed it.

We lay in our cell for many days. The door opened twice each day, once for the men who brought us our bread and water, and once for the Judges. Many Judges came to our cell, first the humblest and then the most honoured Judges of the City. They stood before us in their white togas, and they asked:

"Are you ready to speak?"

But we shook our head, lying before them on the floor. And they departed.

~~And as we lay alone through hours with~~

~~our end, we thought that our brothers had done right. We know no anger against our brothers, and no hatred. We knew we had deserved the lash and the cell and the agony of our body. Yet our curse and the Light born of our curse kept our lips sealed.~~

We counted each day and each night as it passed. Then, to-night, we knew that we must escape. For to-morrow the World Council of Scholars is to meet in our City.

It was easy to escape from the Palace of Corrective Detention. The locks are old on the ~~cell~~ doors and there are no guards about. There is no reason to have guards, for never ~~have men~~ defied the Councils so far as to escape from whatever place they were ordered to be. Our body is healthy and strength returns to it speedily. We lunged against the door and it gave way. We stole through the dark passages, and through the dark streets, and down into our tunnel.

We lit the candle and we saw that our

85

place had not been found and nothing had been touched. And our glass box stood before us on the cold oven, as we had left it. What matter they now, the scars upon our back!

To-morrow, in the full light of day, we shall take our box, and leave our tunnel open, and walk through the streets to the Home of the Scholars. We shall put before them the greatest gift ever ~~laid at the feet of mankind.~~ We shall tell them the truth. We shall hand to them, as our confession, these pages we have written. We shall join our hands to theirs, and we shall work together, with the power of the sky, for the ~~joy and the might and the~~ glory of mankind. Our blessing upon you, our brothers! To-morrow, you will take us back into your fold and we shall be an outcast no longer. To-morrow we shall be one of you again. To-morrow . . .

VII

It is dark here in the forest. The leaves rustle over our head, black against the last gold the sky. The moss is soft. We shall sleep upon this moss for many nights, till the beasts of the forest come to tear our body. We have no bed now, save the moss, and no future, save the beasts.

We are old now, yet we were young this morning, when we carried our box through the streets of the City to the Home of the Scholars. No men stopped us, for there were none about from the Palace of Corrective Detention, and the others knew nothing. No men stopped us at the gate. We walked through empty passages and into the great hall where the World Council of Scholars sat in solemn meeting. We saw nothing as we entered, save the sky in the great windows, blue and glowing. Then we saw the Scholars who sat around a long table; they were as ~~shadows against the light, as~~ shapeless clouds huddled at the rise of the great sky. There were strange men there, men with white skin like ours, and men with black skin, and men with yellow skin, all dressed alike in ~~their~~ white togas. There were men whose famous names we knew, and others from distant lands ~~whom we knew not~~. We saw a great painting ~~which hung~~ on the wall over their heads, of the twenty illustrious men who had invented the candle.

All the heads of the Council turned to us as we entered. ~~And~~ these great and wise of the earth ~~knew not~~ what to think of us, and they looked upon us with ~~puzzlement~~ and ~~curiosity~~, as if we were a miracle ~~which passed understanding~~. It is true that our tunic was torn and stained with brown stains which had been blood. We raised our right arm and we said:

"Our greeting to you, our honored brothers of the World Council of Scholars!"

Then Collective 0-0009, the oldest and wisest of the Council, spoke and they asked:

"Who are you, our brother? For you do not look as a Scholar."

"Our name is Equality 7-2521," we answered, "and we are a Street Sweeper of this City."

Then it was as if a great wind had stricken the hall, and all the Scholars spoke at once, and they were angry and frightened.

"A Street Sweeper! A Street Sweeper walking in upon the World Council of Scholars! It is not to be conceived! It is against all the rules and all the laws!"

But we knew how to stop them.

"Our brothers!" we cried. "We matter not, nor our transgression. It is only our brother men who matter. Give no thought to us, for we are nothing, but listen to our words, for we bring you a gift such as has never been brought to men. Listen to us, for we hold the future of mankind in our hands."

Then they listened.

We placed our box upon the table before them. We spoke of it, and of our long quest, and of our tunnel, and of our escape from the Palace of Corrective Detention. Not a hand moved in that hall, as we spoke, nor an eye. Then we put the wires to the box, and they all bent forward and sat still, watching. And we stood still, our eyes upon the wire. And slowly, slowly as a flush of blood, a red flame trembled in the wire. Then the wire glowed. ~~It glowed! It glowed like a star fallen from heaven upon the Council table.~~

But terror struck the men of the Council. They leapt to their feet, ~~and~~ they ran from the table, and they stood pressed against the wall, huddled together, seeking the warmth of one another's bodies to give them courage.

We looked upon them and we and said:

"Fear nothing, our brothers. There is a great power in these wires, but this power is tamed. It is yours. We give

Still they would not move.

"We give you the power of the sky!" we cried. "We give you the key to the earth! Take it, and let us be one of you, the humblest among you. Let us work together ~~and wring all their secrets from these~~ harness this power and make it ease the toil of men. Let us our candles and our torches. Let us flood our cities with Let us bring a new light to men!"

But they looked upon us, and suddenly we were afraid. For their eyes were still, and small, and evil.

"Our brothers!" we cried. "Have you nothing to say to us?"

Then Collective 0-0009 moved to the table and the others followed, and their eyes upon us were as hungry dogs closing in on their prey.

"Yes," spoke Collective 0-0009, "we have much to say unto you."

And the sound of their voice brought silence to the hall and to the beat of our heart.

"Yes," said Collective 0-0009, "we have much to say to a wretch who have broken all the laws and who glory in their infamy! You scum of the swine! Dare you think that your paltry little mind holds greater wisdom than the minds of your brothers? And if the Councils had decreed that you should be a Street Sweeper, how dared you think that you could be of greater use to men than in sweeping the streets?"

"How dared you, gutter cleaner," spoke

Fraternity 9-3452, "to hold yourself as one alone and with the thoughts of the one and not of the many?"

"~~This renegade~~ shall be burned at the stake," said ~~Equality~~ 4-6998.

"No, they shall be lashed," said Unanimity 7-3304, "till there is nothing left under the lashes."

"No," said Collective 0-0009, "we cannot decide upon this, our brothers. No such crime has ever been committed, and it is not for us to judge. Nor for any small Council. We shall deliver this ~~monster~~ to the World Council itself and let their will be done."

We looked upon them and we pleaded:

"Our brothers! You are right. Let the will of the Council be done upon our body. We ~~care not~~. But the Light? ~~The Light?~~ What will you do with the Light?"

Collective 0-0009 looked upon us, and ~~they rubbed their chin with their fingers,~~ ~~and~~ they smiled.

"So you think that you have found a new power," said Collective 0-0009. "Do all your brothers think that?"

"No," we answered.

"What is not thought by all men cannot be true," said Collective 0-0009.

"You have worked ~~up~~on this alone?" asked International 1-5537.

"Yes," we answered.

"What is not done collectively cannot be good," said International 1-5537.

"Many men in the Homes of the Scholars have had strange new ~~thoughts~~ ideas in the past," said Solidarity 8-1164, "but when the majority of their brother Scholars voted against them, they abandoned their ~~mistaken~~ ideas, as all ~~good~~ men must."

"This box is ~~nothing but foul and~~ useless," ~~magic,"~~ said Alliance 6-7349.

"Should it be what they claim of it," said Harmony 9-2642, "then it would bring ruin to the Department of Candles. The Candle is a great boon to mankind, as approved by all men. Therefore it cannot be destroyed by the whim of one."

"This would wreck the Plans of the World Council," said Unanimity 2-9913, "and without the Plans of the World Council the ~~earth~~ cannot ~~turn~~. It took fifty years to secure the approval of all the Councils for the Candle, and to decide upon the number of candles needed, and to re-fit the Plans so as to make candles instead of torches. This touched upon thousands and thousands of men working in scores of States. We cannot alter the Plans again so soon."

"And if this should lighten the toil of men," said Similarity 5-0306, "then it is a great evil, for men have no cause to exist save in toiling for other men. ~~And evils unspeakable would come upon earth, if men had free time left to them.~~"

Then Collective 0-0009 rose and pointed their finger at our box.

g 95

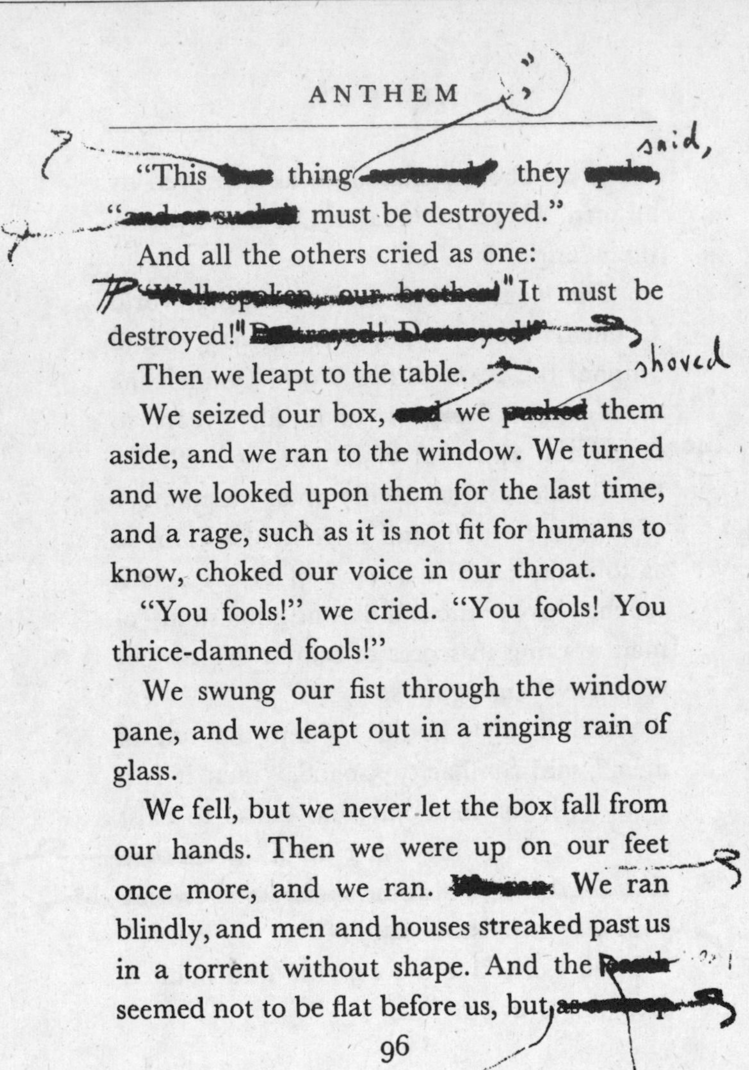

"This thing said, they
" must be destroyed."

And all the others cried as one:

"It must be destroyed!"

Then we leapt to the table.

We seized our box, we shoved them aside, and we ran to the window. We turned and we looked upon them for the last time, and a rage, such as it is not fit for humans to know, choked our voice in our throat.

"You fools!" we cried. "You fools! You thrice-damned fools!"

We swung our fist through the window pane, and we leapt out in a ringing rain of glass.

We fell, but we never let the box fall from our hands. Then we were up on our feet once more, and we ran. We ran blindly, and men and houses streaked past us in a torrent without shape. And the road seemed not to be flat before us, but, as if it were leaping up

~~shaft, and we were flying down the side of this shaft, and the road leapt up~~ to meet us, and we waited for the earth to rise and strike us in the face. But we ran. We knew not where we were going. We knew only that we must run, ~~run,~~ run to the end of the world, to the end of our days.

Then we knew suddenly that we were lying ~~up~~on a soft earth and that we had stopped. Trees taller than we had ever seen stood over us in a great silence. Then we knew. We were in the Uncharted Forest. We had not thought of coming here, but our legs had carried our wisdom, and our legs had brought us to the Uncharted Forest ~~without~~ our will.

Our glass box lay beside us. We crawled to it, we fell upon it ~~with our breast,~~ our face in our arms, and we lay still. ~~We heard no sound save the panting of our breath.~~

We lay thus for a long time. ~~When we had risen,~~ we rose ~~and~~ took our box and ~~we~~

97

against Then We

walked on into the forest. It mattered not where we went. We knew that men would not follow us, for they never enter the Uncharted Forest. We had nothing to fear from them. The forest disposes of its own victims. This gave us no fear either. Only we wished to be away, away from the City and from the air touches upon the air of the City. So we walked on, our box in our arms, our heart empty.

We are doomed. Whatever days are left to us, we shall spend them alone. And we have heard of the corruption to be found in solitude. We have torn ourselves from the truth which is our brother men, and there is no road back for us, and no redemption.

We know these things, but we care. We care for nothing upon earth. We are

Only the box, our arms, is like a living heart which gives us strength.

We have lied to ourselves. We have not built this box for the good of our brothers. We built it for its own sake. It is above all our brothers to us, and its truth above their truth. Why wonder about this? We have not many days to live. We are walking to the fangs awaiting us somewhere among the great, silent trees. There is not a thing behind us to regret.

Then a blow of pain struck us, our first and our only. We thought of the Golden One. We thought of the Golden One whom we shall never see again. Then the pain passed. It is best. We are one of the Damned. It is best if the Golden One forget our name and the body which bore that name.

~~CHAPTER~~

VIII

~~STRANGE are the ways of life. We understand them not,~~ nor ~~the meaning hidden behind them.~~

It has been a day of wonder, this, our first day in the forest. We awoke when a ray of ~~light~~ fell across our face. We ~~wished~~ to leap to our feet, as we have had to leap every morning of our life, but we remembered suddenly that no bell had rung and that there was no bell to ring anywhere. We lay ~~up~~on our back, ~~and~~ we threw our arms out, and we looked up at the sky. The leaves had edges of ~~molten~~ silver ~~which~~ trembled and rippled ~~and sparkled like~~ a river of green and fire flowing high above us. ~~Through the leaves, we saw the sky, blue and clean.~~

100

We ~~wished~~ not to move, ~~our hands sunken in the moss~~. We thought suddenly that we could lie thus as long as we wished, and we laughed aloud at the thought. We could also rise, ~~if we chose~~, or run, or leap, or fall down again. We were thinking that these were thoughts without sense, but before we knew it our body had risen in one leap. Our arms stretched out of their own will, and our body whirled and whirled, till it raised a wind to rustle through the leaves of the bushes. Then our hands seized a branch and swung ~~our body up~~ into a tree, with no aim save the wonder of learning ~~how strong and supple~~ our body ~~was~~. The branch snapped under us and we fell upon the moss soft as a cushion. Then our body, losing all sense, rolled over and over ~~upon~~ the moss, dry leaves in our tunic, in our hair, in our face. And we heard suddenly that we were laughing, laughing aloud, laughing as if there were no power left in us save laughter.

¶ Then we took our glass box, and we

~~We stopped, and we brushed the leaves off our faces, and we said to ourselves that we knew not our body any longer, nor could we understand it. So we came back to our box and lifted it in our arms and~~ went on into the forest. We went on, cutting through the branches, and it was as if we were swimming through a ~~trembling~~ sea of leaves, with the bushes as waves rising and falling and rising around us, and flinging their green sprays high to the tree tops. The trees parted before us, calling us forward. The forest seemed to ~~smile and~~ welcome us. ~~We should have thought otherwise, but our body cried to us that there was no danger and no fangs awaiting us.~~ We went on, without thought, without care, with nothing to feel save the ~~wild~~ song of our body.

We stopped when we felt hunger. ~~We watched this with curiosity. We had never known hunger save as a word.~~ We saw ~~many~~ birds in the tree branches, and flying from under our ~~very~~ footsteps. We picked a stone and we sent it as an arrow at a bird. Our aim is good. The bird fell before us, ~~and quivered, and lay still~~. We made a fire, we cooked the bird, and we ate it, and no meal had ever tasted better to us. And we thought suddenly that there was a great satisfaction to be found in the food which we need and obtain by our own hand. And we wished to be hungry again and soon, that we might know again this strange new pride in eating.

Then we walked on. And we came to a stream which lay as a streak of glass among the trees. It lay so still that we saw no water but only a cut in the earth, in which the trees grew down, upturned, and the sky lay at the bottom. We knelt by the stream and we bent down to drink. And then we stopped. For, upon the blue of the sky below, we saw our own face for the first time.

We sat still and we held our breath ~~not to frighten the picture away~~. For our face and we felt no pity when looking

our body were beautiful. Our face was not like the faces of our brothers, for ~~it gave us no shame to look~~ upon it. Our body was not like the bodies of our brothers, for our limbs were straight and hard and strong. And we thought that we could trust this being who looked upon us from the stream, and that we had nothing to fear with this being. ~~And we threw our head back in a pride senseless and unreasoning~~.

~~Never have men worn adornments of any kind, for it is evil to adorn one among the others. But we gathered leaves and twigs, there, by the stream, and we wove a wreath of them. We know not how such a thought came to us. But we put the wreath upon our head and we looked into the water. And we thought that it was beautiful. Then we said to ourselves that we were vain and foolish, so we threw the wreath away, and we left the stream, and walked on.~~

~~And now that the~~ sun has set ~~and the~~

104

We walked on till the sun had set. When the

And suddenly, for the first time this day, we remembered that we are the Damned. We remembered it, and we laughed.

ed

shadows gather among the trees, we ~~have~~ stopped in a ~~warm little~~ hollow between the roots, where we shall sleep to-night. We are writing this ~~upon~~ on the ~~last of the~~ paper we had hidden in our tunic together with the written pages we had brought for the World Council of Scholars, but never given to them. ~~In the days to come, we shall gather the long, white strips of tree bark which we have seen, and we shall write upon them with charred sticks.~~ We have much to speak of to ourselves, and we hope we shall find the words for it in the days to come. Now, we cannot speak, for we cannot understand.

~~[illegible] which has passed. We know [illegible] [illegible] understand [illegible] they give us the [illegible]~~

For we needed no words to remember that which has happened to us.

~~CHAPTER~~
IX

We have not written for many days. We did not wish ~~at first~~ to speak ~~nor to think.~~ ~~And now it matters not if we write, for that which we are writing to remember can never be forgotten, even without words.~~

It was on our second day in the forest that we heard steps behind us. ~~We stopped and stood still and listened. We heard leaves crackling, far away, softly, steadily, as under no tread of beast or bird.~~ We ~~leapt~~ hid in~~to~~ the ~~thick~~ bushes, ~~and we crouched low,~~ and we waited. The steps came closer. And then we saw the fold of a white tunic among the trees, and a gleam of gold.

~~And then~~ We leapt forward, ~~and~~ we ran

106

to~~ward~~ them, and we stood looking upon the Golden One.

They saw us, and their hands closed into fists, and the fists pulled their arms down ~~taut ropes~~, as if they wished their arms to hold them ~~up~~, while their body swayed. And they ~~looked upon us, and they~~ could not speak.

We dared not come too close to them. We asked, and ~~we had no power over~~ our voice ~~that~~ trembled:

"How come you to be here, Golden One?"

But they ~~heard not our question, for they~~ whispered only:

"We have found you . . . ~~We have found you . . . We have found you.~~"

"How come you to be in the forest?" we asked.

~~Then t~~They raised their head, and ~~their voice was humble but~~ there was a great pride in their ~~eyes, and~~ they answered:

"We have followed you."

~~Then~~ we could not speak, and they said:

107

"We heard that you had gone to the Uncharted Forest, for the whole City is speaking of it. So on the night of the day when we heard it, we ran away from the Home of the Peasants. We found the ~~prints~~ [marks] of your feet across the plain where no men walk. So we followed them, and we went into the forest, and we followed the path where the branches were broken by your ~~passing~~ [body.]"

Their white tunic was torn, and ~~their bare arms were scratched. But there was no weariness in their body, and no fear.~~

"We have followed you," they said, "and we shall follow you wherever you go. If danger threatens you, we shall face it also. If it be death, we shall die with you. You are damned, and we wish to share your damnation." ~~Rather shall we be damned with you than blessed with all our brothers upon this earth."~~

~~And they spoke on, and their head was bowed.~~

108

[the branches had cut the skin of their arms, but they spoke as if they had never taken notice of it, nor of weariness, nor of fear.]

brothers have neither hope nor fire. Your mouth is cut of granite,

~~"We have come to you," they said, "for we have no will but your will, and no thought but your thought, and no breath save the breath you give us. We have come for you are our master, and we cannot leave you."~~ was low, but there was bitterness and triumph in their voice:

~~Then~~ They ~~raised their head, and~~ looked upon us, and ~~their voice~~ ~~[illegible]~~

~~"You are strong and you are beautiful.~~

"Your eyes are as a flame, but our ~~earth is dark and ugly. Your lips are a command,~~ but our brothers are soft and ~~humble. Your body is straight as a spear, and hard as granite, but our brothers are meek and obedient~~. Your head is high, but our brothers cringe. You walk, but our brothers crawl. ~~We spit upon all our brothers, for they are not like you. You are one, alone and only. We have lived for thirty-three days without the sight of you, and we have known the death of our heart. So we came to you, for we knew we must come.~~ We wish to be damned with you, rather than ~~be~~ blessed with all our brothers. Do as you please with us, ~~our master,~~ but do not send us away from you."

Then they knelt, and their golden head ~~was bowed~~ before us, ~~and their hands lay at our feet, palms up, limp and pleading.~~

We had never thought of that which we did. We bent to raise the Golden One to their feet, but when ~~our hands~~ touched ~~their body,~~ it was as if madness had stricken us. We seized their body ~~in our arms~~ and we pressed our lips to theirs. The Golden One breathed once, and their breath was a moan, and then their arms closed around ~~our body.~~

We stood ~~thus~~ together for a long time. And we were frightened that we had lived for twenty-one years and had never known what joy is possible to men.

Then we said:

"Our dearest, ~~our only~~ one. Fear nothing of the forest. There is no danger ~~fears,~~ and no death. ~~We shall guard you, and shield~~

~~you from all anguish~~. We have no need ~~and~~ ~~no wish for~~ our brothers. Let us forget their good and our evil, let us forget all things save that we are together and that there is joy as a bond between us. Give us your hand. ~~[illegible]~~ Look ahead. It is our own world, Golden One, a strange, unknown world, but our own."

Then we walked on into the forest, their hand in ours.

And that night we knew that to hold the body of women in our arms is neither ugly nor shameful, but the ecstasy ~~[illegible]~~ granted to the ~~human~~ race.

We have walked ~~on~~ for many days. The forest has no end, and we seek no end. But each day added to the chain of days between us and the City is like an added blessing. We have made a ~~strong~~ bow and many arrows. We can kill more ~~beasts and~~ birds than we need for our food, ~~and~~ we find water in the forest, ~~and fruit and berries and mush-~~ h

~~[illegible]~~ At night, we choose a ~~small~~ clearing, and we build a ring of fires around it. We sleep in the midst of that ring, and the beasts dare not attack us. We can see their ~~bright little~~ eyes, green and yellow~~, gleaming~~ as coals, watching us from the tree branches ~~and from the bushes~~ beyond. The fires smoulder ~~gently~~ as a crown of jewels around us, and smoke stands still in the air, in ~~misty gray~~ columns, [made] blue ~~and rippling faintly where~~ [by] the moonlight ~~falls upon them~~. We sleep together in the midst of the ring, the arms of the Golden One around us, their head upon our breast.

~~We know not where we are going.~~ Some day, we shall stop and build a house ~~to live in~~ when we shall have gone far enough. But we do not have to hasten. The days before us are without end, ~~as~~ [like] the forest. ~~Now, we wish not to disturb the miracle which is our life, and the joy of our life.~~

~~Nothing is clear to us, yet everything~~

¶ We cannot understand this new life which we have found, yet it seems so clear and so simple. When ~~strange thoughts~~ come to puzzle us, we walk fast ~~and~~ turn ~~to~~ forget all things as we watch the Golden One following. The shadows of leaves fall upon their arms, as they spread the branches apart, but their shoulders are in the sun. The skin of their arms is ~~as~~ a ~~soft~~ blue mist, but their shoulders are ~~as a glowing marble~~, white and ~~transparent~~, as if the light fell not from above, but rose from under their skin. We watch the ~~little~~ leaf which has fallen upon their shoulder, and it lies ~~sealed~~ at the curve of their neck, and a drop of dew glistens ~~as a spark~~ upon it. They approach us, and they stop, ~~and their eyes worship us in silence,~~ and they wait obediently, without questions, till it pleases us to turn and go on.

We go on and we bless the earth under our feet. But questions come to us, ~~again~~ ~~and~~ again, as we walk in silence. If that which we have found is the corruption of

solitude, then what can men wish save corruption? If this is the great evil of being alone, then what is good and what is evil? ~~Yet all truth comes from all men.~~ Everything which comes from ~~all~~ is good. Everything which comes from one is evil. Thus have we been taught with our first breath. We have broken the law, but we have never doubted it. Yet now, ~~now~~ as we walk through the forest, ~~a great doubt rises in our heart.~~

There is no life for men, save in ~~the~~ useful toil for the good of all their brothers. But we lived not, when we toiled for our brothers, we were only weary. There is no joy for men, save the joy shared with all their brothers. But the only ~~two~~ things which ~~set our soul on fire are~~ the power we created in our ~~glass box~~ and the Golden One. And both these joys belong to us alone, ~~and~~ concern ~~not~~ our brothers in any way. Thus do we wonder.

There is some error, ~~immense and~~ ...

~~114~~

the many

we are learning to doubt.

taught us joy were

wires,

they come from us alone, they ~~bear~~ no relation to our brothers, and they do not

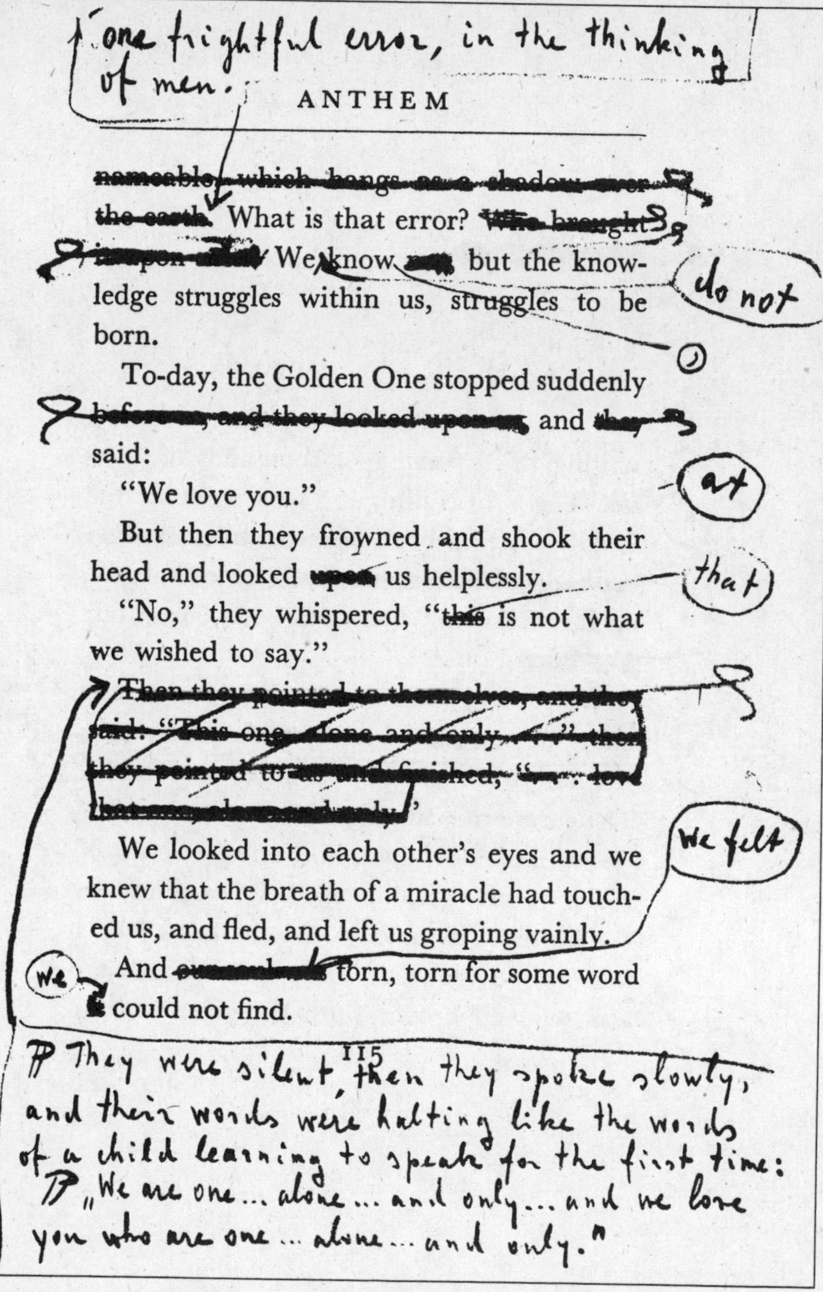

one frightful error, in the thinking of men.

ANTHEM

~~nameable, which hangs as a shadow over the earth.~~ What is that error? ~~Who brought it upon men?~~ We do not know, ~~...~~ but the knowledge struggles within us, struggles to be born.

To-day, the Golden One stopped suddenly ~~before us, and they looked upon us,~~ and ~~they~~ said:

"We love you."

But then they frowned and shook their head and looked ~~upon~~ at us helplessly.

"No," they whispered, "~~this~~ that is not what we wished to say."

~~Then they pointed to themselves, and they said: "This one ... alone and only ...," then they pointed to us unfinished, "... love that one, alone and only."~~

We looked into each other's eyes and we knew that the breath of a miracle had touched us, and fled, and left us groping vainly. We felt

And ~~our words were~~ torn, torn for some word we could not find.

115

¶ They were silent, then they spoke slowly, and their words were halting like the words of a child learning to speak for the first time:

¶ "We are one ... alone ... and only ... and we love you who are one ... alone ... and only."

X

We are sitting at a table and writing this upon paper thousands of years . The light is dim, and we cannot see the Golden One, only one lock of gold on the pillow of an ancient bed. This is our home.

We came upon it to-day, at sunrise. For many days, we had been crossing a mountain The forest rose among cliffs, and whenever we walked out upon a barren stretch of rock, we saw great peaks before us, and to the north of us, and to the south, as far as our eyes could see. The peaks red and brown, with the green streaks

116

of forests as veins upon them, with blue mists as crowns over their heads. We had never heard of these mountains, nor seen them marked on any map. The Uncharted Forest has protected them from the Cities and the men of the Cities.

We ~~went on~~, climbi~~ng~~ paths where the wild goat dared not ~~[illegible]~~. ~~We hung over chasms without bottom~~. Stones rolled from under our feet, and we heard them striking the rock below, ~~again and again~~, farther and farther down, and the mountains rang ~~and rang~~ with each ~~blow~~, and long after the ~~sounds~~ had died. But we went on, for we knew that no men would follow our track nor reach us here. ~~Our tunics and sandals had long since fallen to shreds. We both wore the skins of the beasts we had killed; we carried our bow and arrows over one shoulder, and the glass box with the power of the sky in our arms.~~

Then to-day, at sunrise, we saw a white

117

among the trees, high on a sheer peak before us. We thought that it was a fire and we. But was un-moving blinding as liquid . So we climbed toward it through the rocks. And there, before us, on a broad summit, with the mountains rising behind it, stood a house such as we had never seen, and the white came from the sun on the glass of its windows.

The house had two stories and a strange roof flat as a floor. there was more window than wall upon its walls, and the windows straight around the corners, though how this kept the house standing we could not ~~window frames were not of wood, but of a blue metal, which felt like iron, but it was~~ the walls were hard and smooth, of that stone unlike stone which we had seen in our tunnel.

We both knew it without words: this

118

house was left from the Unmentionable Times. The trees had protected it from time and weather, and from men who have less pity than time and weather. the Golden One and we asked:

"Are you afraid?"

But they shook their head. So we walked to the door, and we threw it open and we stepped together into the house of the Unmentionable Times.

We shall need the days and the years ~~before us~~ to look, to learn and to understand the things of this house. To-day we could only look and try to believe the sight of our eyes. We pulled the heavy curtains from the windows and we saw that the rooms were small, and more than twelve men could have ~~dwelt~~ here ~~which was strange~~. Never had we seen rooms so full of light. ~~They were as bowls which~~

119

We turned to

ahead

we thought that not

lived

We thought it was strange that men had been permitted to build a house for only twelve.

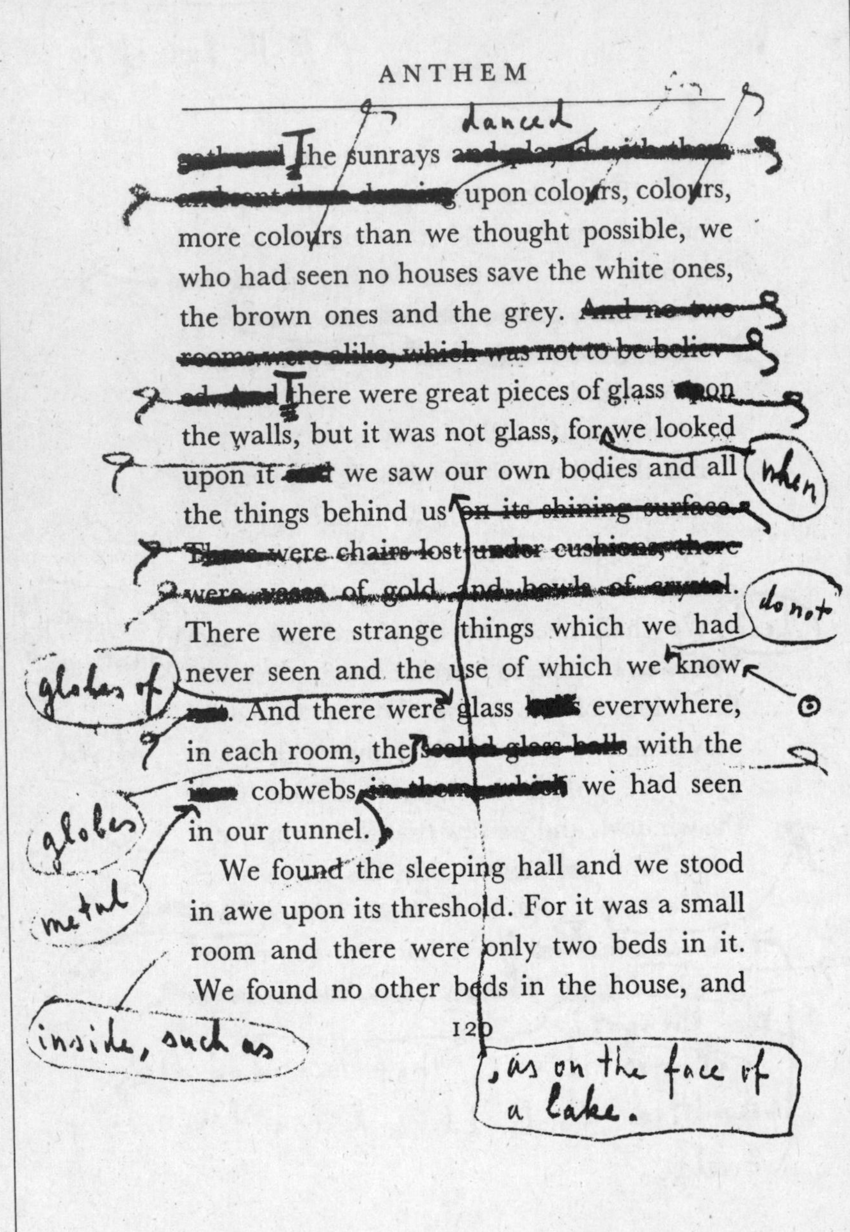

ANTHEM

~~[illegible]~~ the sunrays ~~and played with them~~ ~~and sent them dancing~~ upon colours, colours, more colours than we thought possible, we who had seen no houses save the white ones, the brown ones and the grey. ~~And no two rooms were alike, which was not to be believed. And~~ there were great pieces of glass ~~upon~~ the walls, but it was not glass, for we looked upon it ~~and~~ we saw our own bodies and all the things behind us ~~on its shining surface.~~ ~~There were chairs lost under cushions, there were vases of gold and bowls of crystal.~~ There were strange things which we had never seen and the use of which we know ~~not~~. And there were glass ~~balls~~ everywhere, in each room, the ~~sealed glass balls~~ with the ~~iron~~ cobwebs ~~in them which~~ we had seen in our tunnel.

We found the sleeping hall and we stood in awe upon its threshold. For it was a small room and there were only two beds in it. We found no other beds in the house, and

120

What kind of world did they have, the men of the Unmentionable Times?

then we knew that only two ~~beings~~ had ~~dwelt~~ lived here, and this passes ~~all~~ understanding.

We found garments, rows of garments, and the Golden One gasped at the sight of them. For they were not white tunics, nor white togas; ~~they were of silk and of velvet and of cloth thin as air~~; they were ~~red and blue and golden and of more colours than we could name. And no two garments were~~ of all colors, no two of them alike. Some crumbled to dust as we touched them. But others were of heavier cloth, and they felt soft ~~and bright~~ and new in our fingers.

~~And then~~ We found a room with walls made of shelves, ~~and upon them stood~~ which held rows and rows of manuscripts, from the floor to the ceiling. Never have we seen such a number of them, nor of such strange shape. They were not soft and rolled, they had hard shells of ~~leather and~~ cloth ~~upon them~~ and leather; and the letters on their pages were so small and so even that we wondered at the men who had such handwritings. We glanced through the pages, and we saw that they were written in our language, but we found many words which we could not understand. To-morrow, we shall begin to read these ~~books. We shall read them all. We know not what secrets they may reveal.~~

When we had seen all the rooms of the house, we looked upon the Golden One and ~~they looked upon us, and~~ we knew the thought in our minds.

~~"Never," we said.~~

~~"Never," whispered the Golden One.~~

~~"Never shall we~~ leave this house," we said, "nor let it be taken from us. This is our home and the end of our journey. This is your house, Golden One, and ours, and it belongs to no other men whatever as far as the earth may stretch. We shall not share it with others, as we share not our joy with them, nor our love, nor our hunger. So be it to the end of our days."

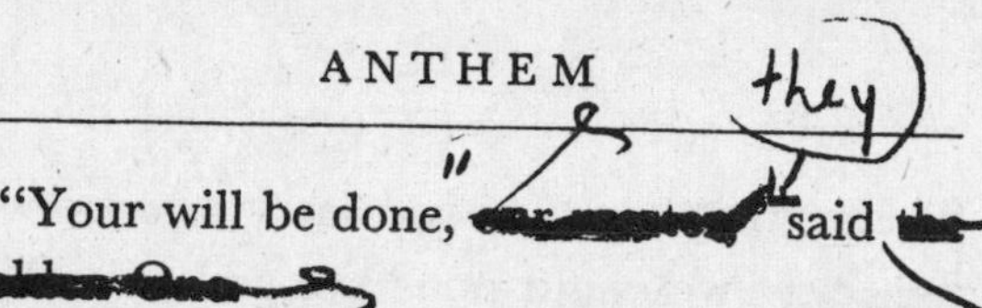

"Your will be done, our master," said the Golden One.

Then we went out to gather wood for the great hearth of our home. We brought water from a stream which runs among the trees under our windows. We killed a mountain goat, and we brought its flesh to be cooked in a strange copper pot we found in a place of wonders, which must have been the cooking room of the house.

We did this work alone, for no words of ours could take the Golden One away from the big glass which is not glass. They stood before it and they looked and looked upon their own body. They had found a small casket in the sleeping room, and it was full of jewels such as no men had ever touched, save upon the great mosaics of the Palace of the World Council. The Golden One put long strings of rubies on their shoulders, and circles of gold upon their arms, and clusters of diamonds on their ears.

123

These things must have been made for such use, only we could not have guessed it, but the Golden One guessed. And they stood before the magic glass, and they looked, and the sun sent fires to dance upon the jewels, and sparks of all colours glittered in the fur which wrapped the body of the Golden One.

We cannot tell all the wonders of this day. And when the sun sank beyond the mountains, we were weary, but this weariness was a delight to us. The Golden One fell asleep on the floor, amidst all the garments they had spread out, amidst jewels, and bottles of crystal, and flowers of silk. We lifted the Golden One in our arms and we carried them to a bed, their head falling softly upon our shoulder, in their sleep. Then we lit a candle, which we had found in the cooking room, and we brought paper from the room of the manuscripts, and we sat by the window, for we knew that we could not sleep to-night.

And now we look upon the earth and sky. This spread of naked rock and peaks and moonlight is like a world ready to be born, a world that waits. It seems to us it asks a sign from us, a spark, a first commandment.

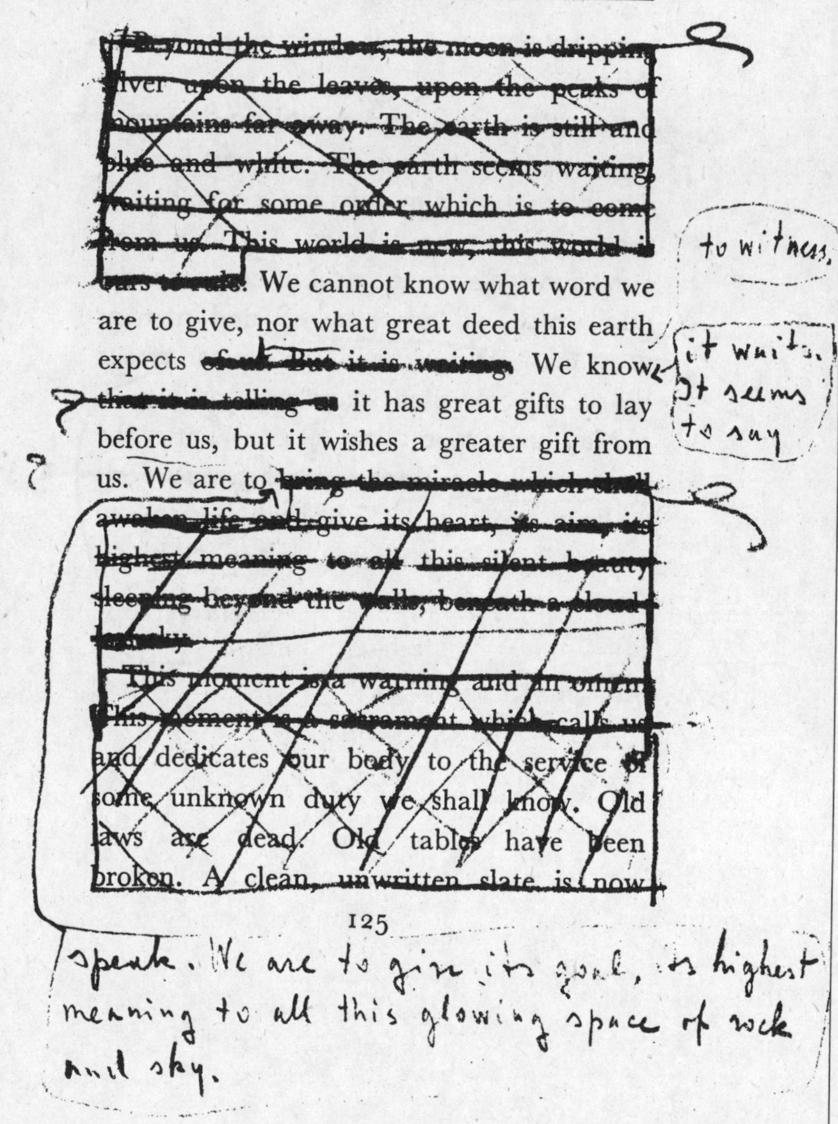

ANTHEM

Beyond the window, the moon is dripping silver upon the leaves, upon the peaks of mountains far away. The earth is still and blue and white. The earth seems waiting, waiting for some order which is to come from us. This world is new, this world is ours to rule. We cannot know what word we are to give, nor what great deed this earth expects of us. But it is waiting. We know that it is telling us it has great gifts to lay before us, but it wishes a greater gift from us. We are to bring the miracle which shall awaken life and give its heart, its aim, its highest meaning to all this silent beauty sleeping beyond the walls, beneath a cloudless sky.

This moment is a warning and an omen. This moment is a sacrament which calls us and dedicates our body to the service of some unknown duty we shall know. Old laws are dead. Old tables have been broken. A clean, unwritten slate is now

125

to witness.

it waits. It seems to say

speak. We are to give its goal, its highest meaning to all this glowing space of rock and sky.

~~lying before our hands. Our fingers are to wise.~~

~~Our heart is still and humble in this hour.~~ We ~~bow our head~~, we beg our ~~soul~~ for guidance in answering this call no voice has spoken, yet we have heard. We look upon our hands. We see the dust of centuries, the dust which hid great secrets and perhaps great evils. And yet it ~~brings~~ no fear ~~to~~ our heart, but only silent reverence and pity.

May knowledge come to us! What is the secret our heart ~~seems to have grasped, but~~ will not reveal to us, although it seems to beat as if it were endeavouring to tell it?

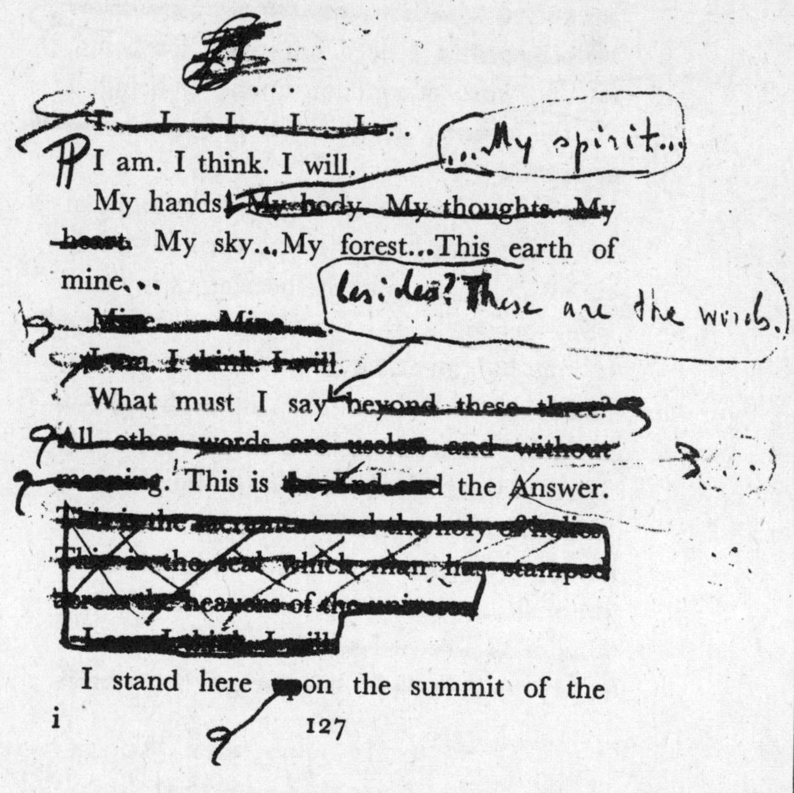

CHAPTER

XI

. . .

I . . . I . . . I . . .

I am. I think. I will.

My hands. My body. My thoughts. My heart. My sky... My forest... This earth of mine...

Mine... Mine...

I am. I think. I will.

What must I say beyond these three? All other words are useless and without meaning. This is the End and the Answer.

This is the sacrament and the holy of holies. This is the seal which man has stamped across the heavens of the universe.

I am. I think. I will.

I stand here upon the summit of the

i 127

I wished to know the meaning of things. I am the meaning. I wished to find a warrant for being.

my

the

warrant

warrant

mountain. I lift my head and I spread my arms. This, ~~this~~ body ~~of mine~~ and ~~this~~ spirit ~~of mine in my body~~, this is the end of ~~all~~ quest. ~~And the air~~ [illegible] ~~Behold, here is the goal and the reason for all things.~~ ~~But~~ I need no ~~reason~~ for being, and no word of sanction upon my being. I am the ~~reason~~ and the sanction. ~~I, my body, my spirit.~~

It is my eyes which see, and the sight of my eyes grants beauty to the earth. It is my ears which hear, and the hearing of my ears gives its song to the world. ~~All things come to my judgment, and I weigh all things, and I seal upon them my "Yes" or my "No." Thus is Truth born. Such is the root of all Truth and the leaf, such is the fount of all Truth and the ocean, such is the base of all Truth and the summit. I am the judge. I am the scale and the weigher. I am the beginning of all Truth. I am its end.~~

~~My road is dark, but the guiding star is~~

It is my mind which thinks, and the judgment of my mind is the only searchlight that can find the truth. It is my will which chooses, and the choice of my will is the only edict I must respect.

within me. The guiding star and the compass with a loadstone which points the way. It points for all eternity in but one direction. It points to me.

I think. My thought is the way, the road and the traveller. My thought is my temple and my fort. My thought is my god, and the priest of me, and the warrior. My thought is my altar and the sword in my hand. I fight not, save by my own hand and with my own sword.

Where I go, there does my will go before me. My will, which chooses, and orders, and creates. My will, the master which knows no masters. My will, the liberator and the conqueror. My will, which is the thin flame, still and holy, in the shrine of my body, my body which is but the shrine of my will. Many words have been granted me, and some are wise, and some are false, but only three are holy: "I will it!"

I know not if this earth upon which I

129

¶ Whatever road I take, the guiding star is within me; the guiding star and the loadstone which point the way. They point for all eternity in but one direction. They point to me.

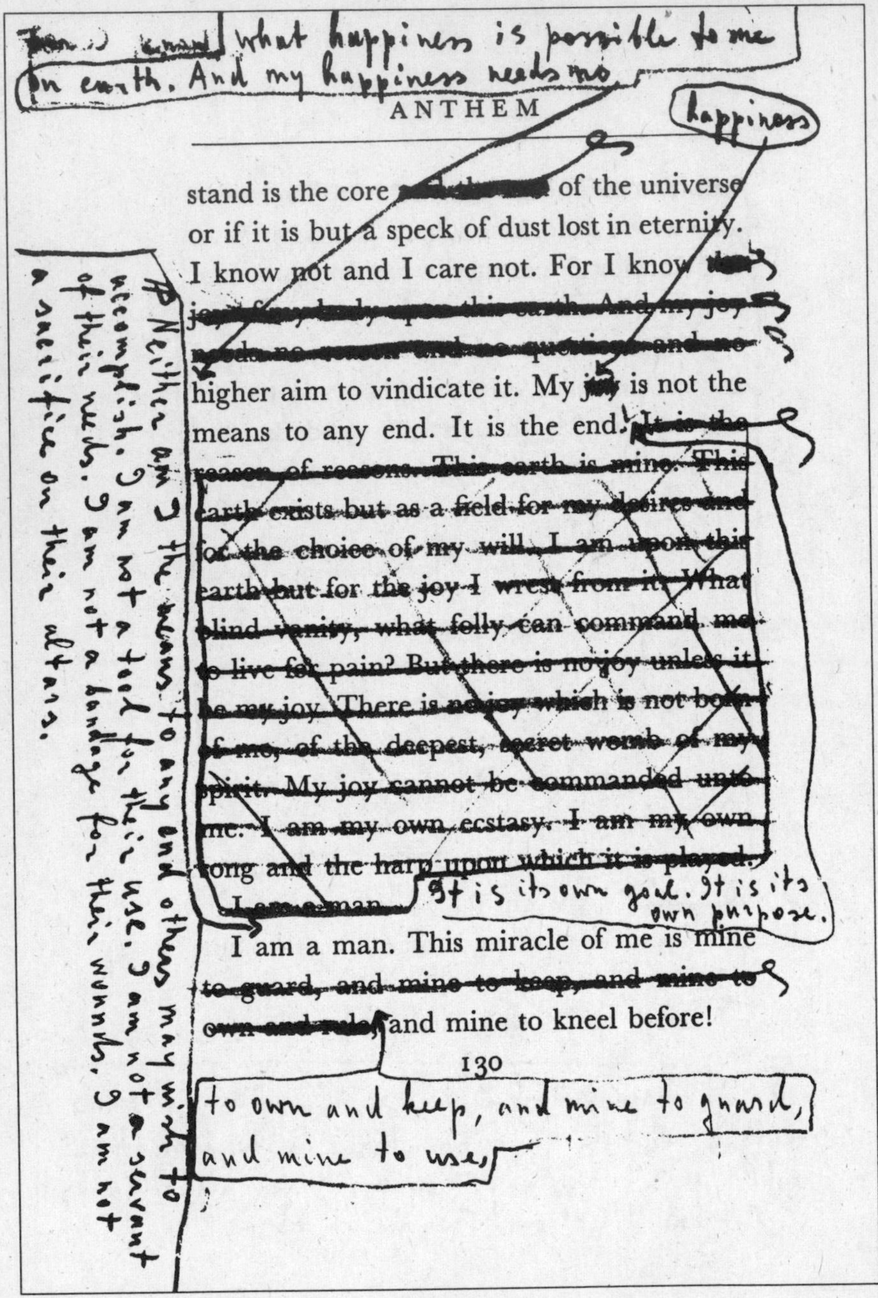

~~[illegible]~~ what happiness is possible to me on earth. And my happiness needs no

ANTHEM

happiness

stand is the core ~~[illegible]~~ of the universe or if it is but a speck of dust lost in eternity. I know not and I care not. For I know ~~[illegible]~~ ~~joy is possible to me upon this earth. And my joy needs no reason and no questions and no~~ higher aim to vindicate it. My ~~joy~~ is not the means to any end. It is the end. ~~It is the reason of reasons. This earth is mine. This earth exists but as a field for my desires and for the choice of my will. I am upon this earth but for the joy I wrest from it. What blind vanity, what folly can command me to live for pain? But there is no joy unless it be my joy. There is no joy which is not born of me, of the deepest, secret womb of my spirit. My joy cannot be commanded unto me. I am my own ecstasy. I am my own song and the harp upon which it is played.~~ It is its own goal. It is its own purpose.

~~I am a man.~~

¶ Neither am I the means to any end others may wish to accomplish. I am not a tool for their use. I am not a servant of their needs. I am not a bondage for their wounds. I am not a sacrifice on their altars.

I am a man. This miracle of me is mine ~~to guard, and mine to keep, and mine to own and rule,~~ to own and keep, and mine to guard, and mine to use, and mine to kneel before!

130

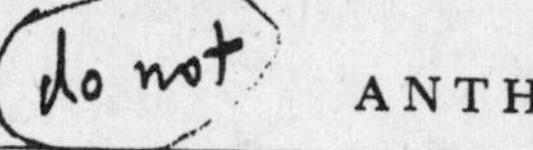

~~And so I hail my will! And so I guard my will before I guard my life. Let no man covet my will and the freedom of my will. Woe to them who have tried!~~

I surrender ~~not~~ my treasures, nor do I share them. The fortune of my spirit is not to be blown into coins of brass and flung to the winds as alms for the poor of the spirit. I guard my treasures: my thought, my will, my freedom. And the greatest of these is freedom.

I owe nothing to my brothers, nor do I gather debts from them. ~~I wish no man to be like me, nor do I wish to be like any man.~~ I ask none to live for me, nor do I live for any others. I covet no man's soul, nor is my soul theirs to covet.

I am neither foe nor friend to my brothers, but such as each of them shall deserve of me. And to earn my love, my brothers must do more than to have been born. ~~[illegible]~~ I grant ~~[illegible]~~ without reason, nor

131

 [friends]

to any chance passer-by who may wish to claim it. I honour men with my love. But honour is a thing to be earned.

I shall choose ~~companions from~~ among ~~my brothers~~ [men,] but neither slaves nor masters. And I shall choose only such as please me, and them I shall ~~honour and~~ love and respect, but neither command nor obey. And we shall join our hands when we wish, or walk alone when we ~~choose~~ [so desire.]. For ~~in his heart of hearts and~~ in the ~~sanctuary~~ [temple] of his spirit, each man is alone. Let each man keep his ~~sanctuary~~ [temple] untouched and undefiled. Then let him join hands with others if he wishes, ~~and there is no shame and no evil in such joining,~~ but only beyond his holy threshold.

~~For great are the evils of this earth, but none so great as the evils which come from men. And the greatest of these lies hidden in one word, and this word is "WE." For this word has a monster hidden in it. This word can escape its master. And when this~~

¶ For the word "WE" must never be spoken, save by one's choice and as a second thought. This word must never be placed first within man's soul, else it becomes a monster, the root of all the evils on earth, the root of man's torture by men, and of an unspeakable lie.

The word "We" is as lime poured over men,

word takes the power over man, then does it bring forth upon earth all of man's sorrows and man's darkest shame. For this word is as a shroud which covers the dead. It is as lime, which sets and hardens like stone, and crushes all beneath it, and that which is white and that which is black are lost equally in the grey of it. It is the word by which the wicked steal the virtue of the good, by which the weak steal the might of the strong, by which the fools steal the wisdom of the sages.

to

depraved

Then darkness descends upon earth, and shame, and a great lie. For one man may be evil, but ten million such as he are called good together. For one man may be foolish, but ten million such as he are called wise together. For one may be a knave, but ten million knaves are called a saint. Then all things become dim and crooked, and reason is shackled that it may not disturb this unreason, and all truth vanishes from the earth.

What is my joy if all hands, even the

creed of corruption.

unclean, can reach into it? What is my wisdom, if even the fools can dictate ~~unto~~ to me? What is my freedom, if all creatures, even the botched and the impotent, are my masters? What is my life, if I am but to bow, to agree and to obey?

But I am done with this ~~reign of folly, for my eyes are opened.~~

~~I have broken the tables of my brothers, and my own tables do I now write for my own spirit.~~

I have destroyed the monster which hung as a black cloud over the earth and hid the sun from man. The monster which sat upon a throne, with chains held in his hands, with his feet upon man's throat, with the blood of man's free spirit for his sustenance. ~~The monster of the word "We."~~

And now I ~~look upon the sacred~~ see the face of god, and ~~this god do~~ this god I raise over the earth, ~~higher than the heavens, brighter than the sun,~~ this god whom men have sought since

134

¶ I am done with the monster of "We," the word of serfdom, of plunder, of misery, falsehood and shame.

men came into being, this god who will grant them joy and peace and pride.

This god, this one word:

"I."

k 135

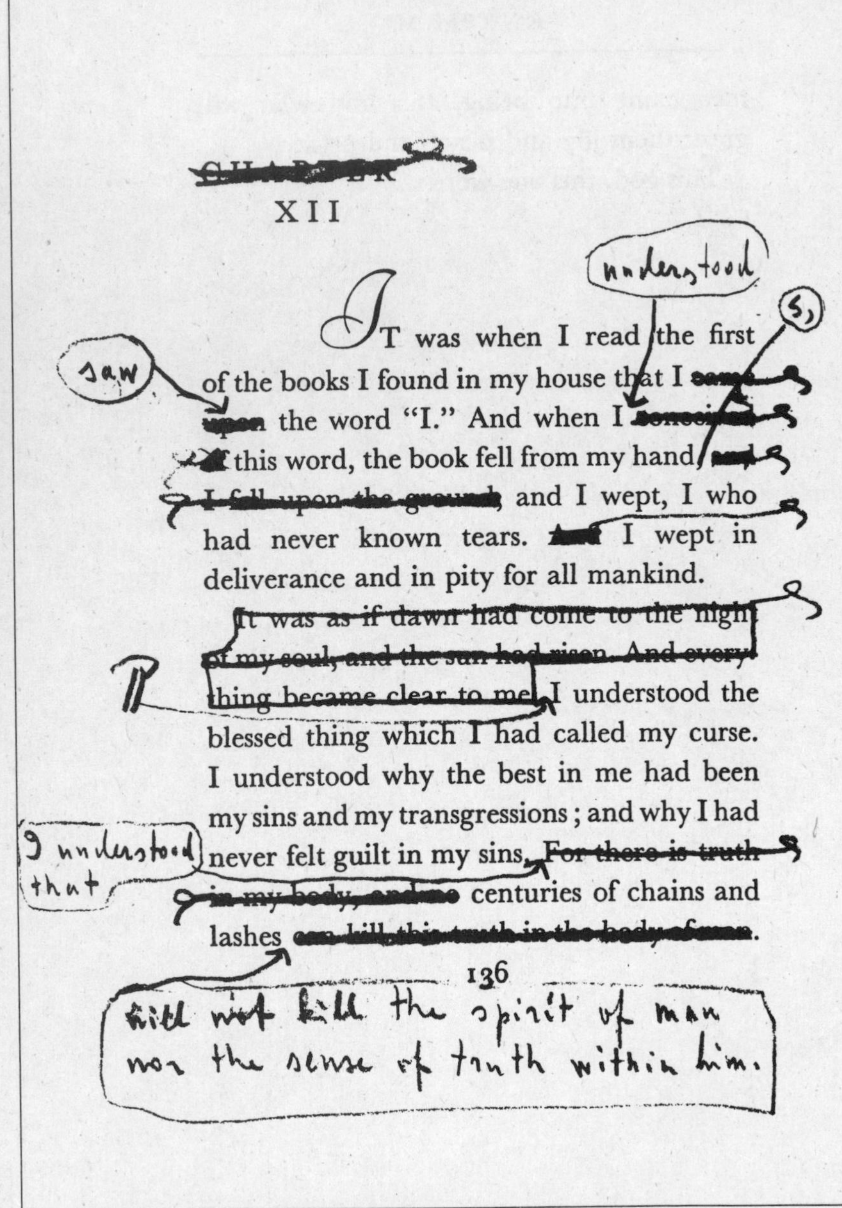

~~CHAPTER~~

XII

IT was when I read the first of the books I found in my house that I ~~came~~ ~~upon~~ the word "I." And when I ~~conceived~~ ~~of~~ this word, the book fell from my hand, ~~and~~ ~~I fell upon the ground,~~ and I wept, I who had never known tears. ~~And~~ I wept in deliverance and in pity for all mankind.

~~It was as if dawn had come to the night of my soul, and the sun had risen. And everything became clear to me.~~ I understood the blessed thing which I had called my curse. I understood why the best in me had been my sins and my transgressions; and why I had never felt guilt in my sins. ~~For there is truth in my body, and no~~ centuries of chains and lashes ~~can kill this truth in the body of man~~.

136

I read many books for many days. Then I called the Golden One and I told her what I had read and what I had learned. She looked me and the first words she spoke were

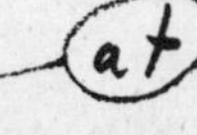

"I love ."

Then I said:

"My dearest one, it is not for men to be without names. There was a time when each man had a name of his own to distinguish him from all other men. So let us choose our names. I have read of a man who lived many thousands of years ago, and of all the names in these books, his is the one I wish to bear. He took the light of the gods and he brought it to men, and he men to be gods. And he suffered for his deed as all bearers of light must suffer. His name was Prometheus."

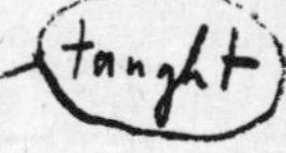

"It shall be name, " said the Golden One.

"And I have read of a goddess," I said,

"who was the mother of the earth and of all the gods. Her name was Gaea. Let this be ~~the~~ name, my Golden One, for ~~we have a new world to build, and thou art~~ to be the mother of a new ~~race~~ of gods."

"It shall be my name," said the Golden One.

Now I look ahead. My future is clear before me. The Saint of the pyre had seen the future when he chose me as his heir, as the heir of all the saints and all the martyrs who came before him and who died for the same cause, for the same word, no matter what name they gave to their cause and their truth. ~~I shall not go back to the City of slaves.~~ I shall live here, in my own house. ~~I shall work the earth of my mountains, and I shall plant seeds, and I shall tend to the fruit trees and the vines, and make them to yield their fruit for my table.~~ I shall take my food from the earth by the toil of my own hands. ~~And the toil of my own hands will~~

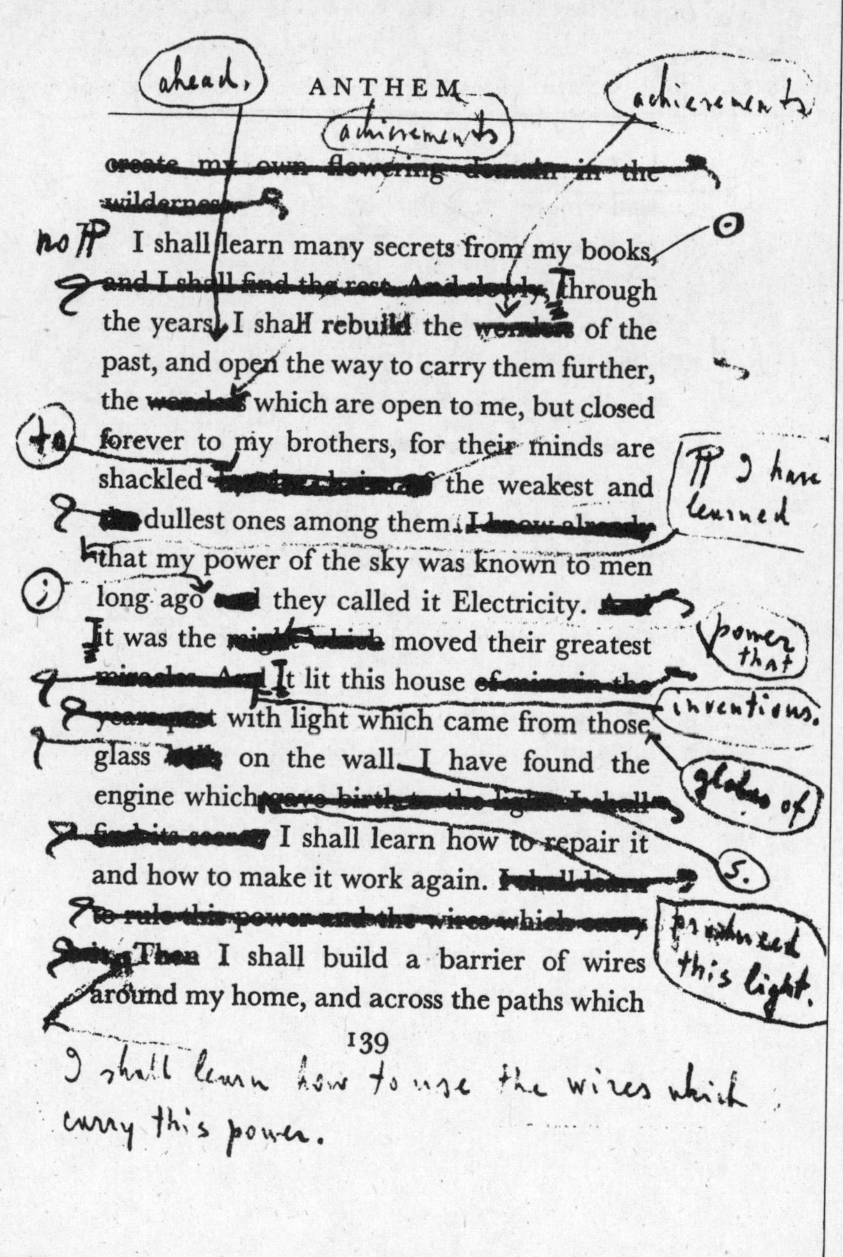
ANTHEM

create my own flowering domain in the wilderness.

I shall learn many secrets from my books, and I shall find the rest. And slowly, through the years, I shall rebuild the wonders of the past, and open the way to carry them further, the wonders which are open to me, but closed forever to my brothers, for their minds are shackled by the chains of the weakest and the dullest ones among them. I know already that my power of the sky was known to men long ago and they called it Electricity. And it was the might which moved their greatest miracles. And it lit this house of mine in the years past with light which came from those glass balls on the wall. I have found the engine which gave birth to the light. I shall find its secret. I shall learn how to repair it and how to make it work again. I shall learn to rule this power and the wires which carry it. Then I shall build a barrier of wires around my home, and across the paths which

139

ahead,
achievements
achievements
no ¶
to
¶ I have learned
;
power that
inventions.
globes of
5.
produced this light.

I shall learn how to use the wires which carry this power.

a barrier my brothers will never be able to cross. For they have nothing to fight me with, save the brute force of their numbers. I have my mind.

lead to my home. A barrier light as a cobweb ~~and~~ more impassable than a wall of granite.

Then here, ~~upon~~ this mountain top, with the world below me and nothing above me ~~save~~ the sun, I shall live my own truth. ~~As a challenge to the lies of my brothers will it be, this life of mine, and as an example.~~ Gaea is pregnant with my child. Our son will be raised as a man. He will be taught to say "I" and to bear the pride of it. He will be taught to walk straight and ~~upon~~ his own feet. He will be taught reverence for his own spirit.

When I shall have read all the books, and learned my new way, when my home will be ready and my earth tilled, I shall steal one day, for the last time, into the cursed City of my birth. I shall call to me my friend who has no name save International 4-8818, and all those like him, Fraternity 2-5503 who cries without reason, and Solidarity 9-6347

who calls for help in the night, and a few others. I shall call to me all the men and the women whose spirits have not been killed within them and who suffer under the yoke of their brothers. They will follow me and I shall lead them to my fortress. And here, in this uncharted wilderness, I and they, my chosen friends, my fellow-builders, shall write the first chapter in the new history of man.

These are the things before me. And as I stand here at the door of glory, I look behind me for the last time. I look upon the history of men, which I have learned from the books, and I wonder. It was a long story, and the spirit which moved it was the spirit of man's freedom. But what is freedom? Freedom from what? There is nothing to take a man's freedom away from him, save other men. So that to be free, a man must be free of his brothers. That is Freedom. That and nothing else. At first, man was enslaved by the gods

~~and by the servants of the gods~~. But he broke their chains. Then he was enslaved by the ~~kings and by the mobs who bowed to the~~ kings. But he broke their chains. He was enslaved by his birth, ~~and~~ by his kin, ~~and~~ by his race. But he broke their chains. He declared ~~un~~to all his brothers that a man has rights which neither god nor king nor other men can take away from him, no matter what their number~~s~~, for his is the right of man, and there is no right on earth above this right. And he stood ~~up~~on the threshold of the freedom for which the blood of the centuries behind him had been spilled.

And then came the twilight.

What brought it to pass? What disaster ~~struck the earth and~~ took their reason away from men? What whip lashed them to their knees in shame and submission? The worship of the word "We." ~~I know not. The books do not speak of it. These books are very old. When the twilight came, men wrote no longer, neither did they read. So~~

142

¶ When men accepted that worship, the structure of centuries collapsed about them,

~~the story of man's fall is dark for ever, dark as the hearts of those who brought it about.~~

~~But when they brought it about, the structure of centuries fell to dust at men's feet,~~ the structure whose every beam had come from the thought of some one man, each in his day down the ages, from the depth of some one spirit, such spirit as existed but for its own sake. Those men who survived—those eager to live for one another, since they had nothing else to vindicate them—those men could neither carry on, nor ~~keep~~ what they had received. Thus did all thought, all science, all wisdom perish on earth. Thus did men—men with nothing to offer save their great number—lose the steel towers ~~and~~ the flying ships ~~and~~ the power wires, which they had ~~never~~ created and could never keep. Perhaps, later, some men had been born with ~~sight~~ and courage to recover these things which were lost; perhaps these men came before the Councils

eager to obey,

preserve

not

the

all the things

the mind

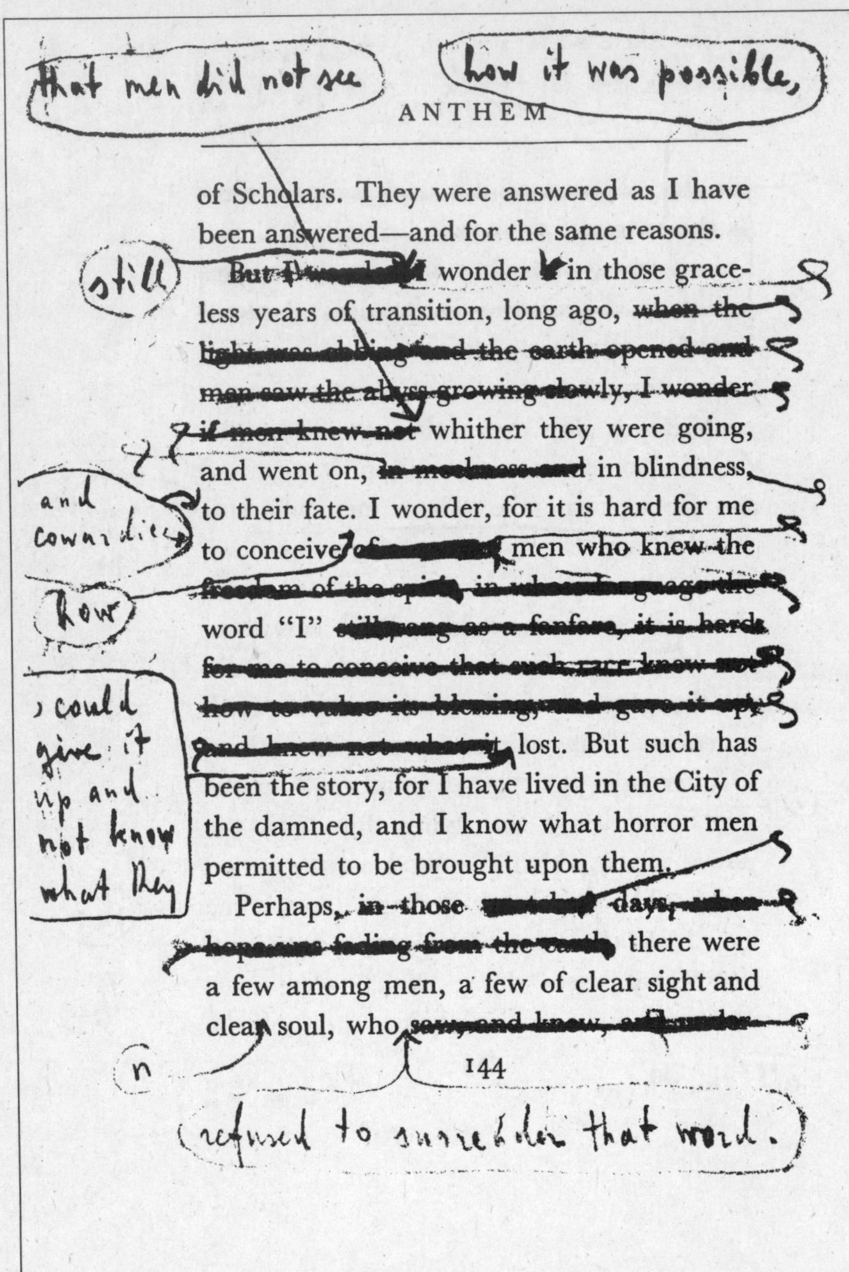

ANTHEM

of Scholars. They were answered as I have been answered—and for the same reasons.

~~But I wonder~~ I wonder ~~if~~ in those graceless years of transition, long ago, ~~when the light was ebbing and the earth opened and men saw the abyss growing slowly, I wonder if men knew not~~ whither they were going, and went on, ~~in meekness and~~ in blindness, to their fate. I wonder, for it is hard for me to conceive ~~of~~ men ~~who knew the freedom of the spirit, in whose language the~~ word "I" ~~still rang as a fanfare, it is hard for me to conceive that such men knew not how to value its blessing, and gave it up, and knew not what it~~ lost. But such has been the story, for I have lived in the City of the damned, and I know what horror men permitted to be brought upon them.

Perhaps, ~~in those days, when hope was fading from the earth~~ there were a few among men, a few of clear sight and clear soul, who ~~saw, and knew~~

144

~~[illegible]~~ What agony must have been theirs before that which they saw coming and could not stop! Perhaps they ~~[illegible]~~ out in protest and in warning. But men paid no heed to their warning. And they, these few, fought a hopeless battle, and they perished with their banners smeared by their own blood. And they chose to perish, for they knew. To them, I send my salute across the centuries, and my pity.

Theirs is the banner in my hand. And I wish I had the power to tell them that the despair of their hearts was not to be ~~[illegible]~~ and their night was not without hope. For the battle they lost can never be lost. For that which they died to save can never perish. Through all the darkness, through all the shame of which men are capable, ~~be it centuries upon centuries of it~~, the spirit of man will remain ~~living upon the~~ earth. It may sleep, but it will awaken. It may wear chains, but it will break through.

And man will go on. Man, not men.

Here, ~~upon my~~ mountain, I and my sons and my chosen friends shall build our new land and our fort. And it will become as the heart of the earth, lost and hidden at first, but beating, ~~[illegible]~~ beating louder each day. And word of it will reach every corner of the earth. And the roads of the world will become as veins which will carry the best of the world's blood to my threshold. And all my brothers, and the Councils of my brothers, will hear of it, but they will be impotent against me. And the day will come, ~~though I may not be here to see it, when my race will conquer the~~ earth, and raze ~~to the ground~~ the cities of the enslaved, and my home will become the capital of a ~~new, free~~ world.

For the coming of that day shall I fight, I and my sons and my chosen friends. For the freedom of Man. For his right. For his honour. ~~[illegible]~~

146

We shall know no fear and no doubt. Ours will be the holy war, the holy, the blessed and the last. We may perish, but our truth will go on. We may fall, but our torch is too bright ever to die again. What if we perish? The first have always perished. But I think not of danger. I look ahead through the years to the sun of my victory. I laugh. I sing to my victory.

And here, over the portals of my fort, I shall cut in the stone the word which is to be our torch and our banner. The word which will give us our blessing and our courage. The word which will not die, should we all perish in battle. The word which can never die on this earth, for it is the heart of it and the spirit and the glory.

The sacred word:

EGO